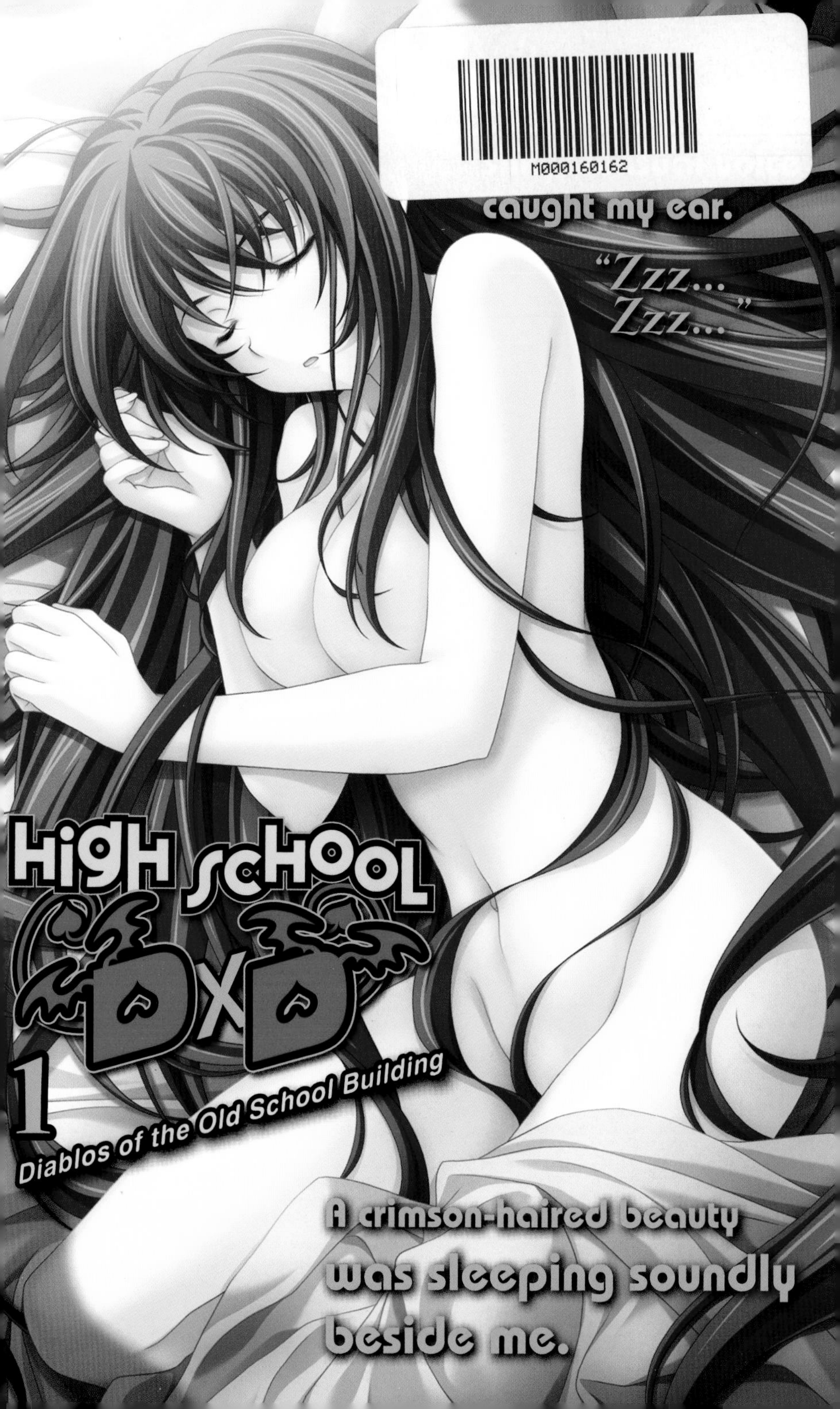
caught my ear.
"Zzz... Zzz..."
HIGH SCHOOL DxD
1
Diablos of the Old School Building
A crimson-haired beauty
was sleeping soundly
beside me.

"...You'll really
be my friend?"

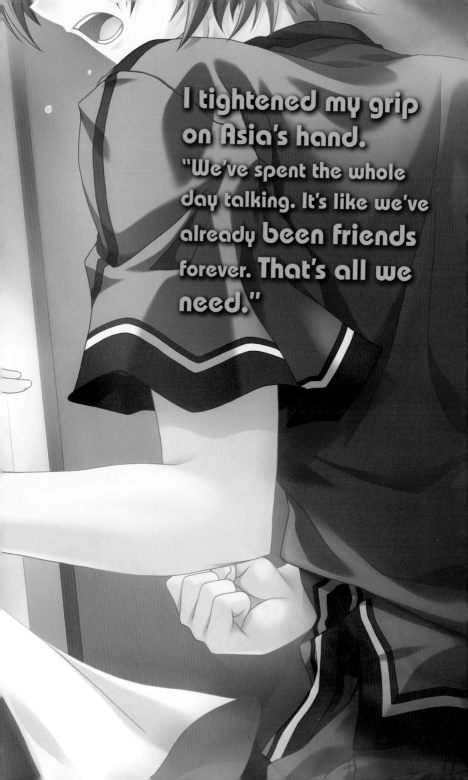

I tightened my grip on Asia's hand.

"We've spent the whole day talking. It's like we've already been friends forever. That's all we need."

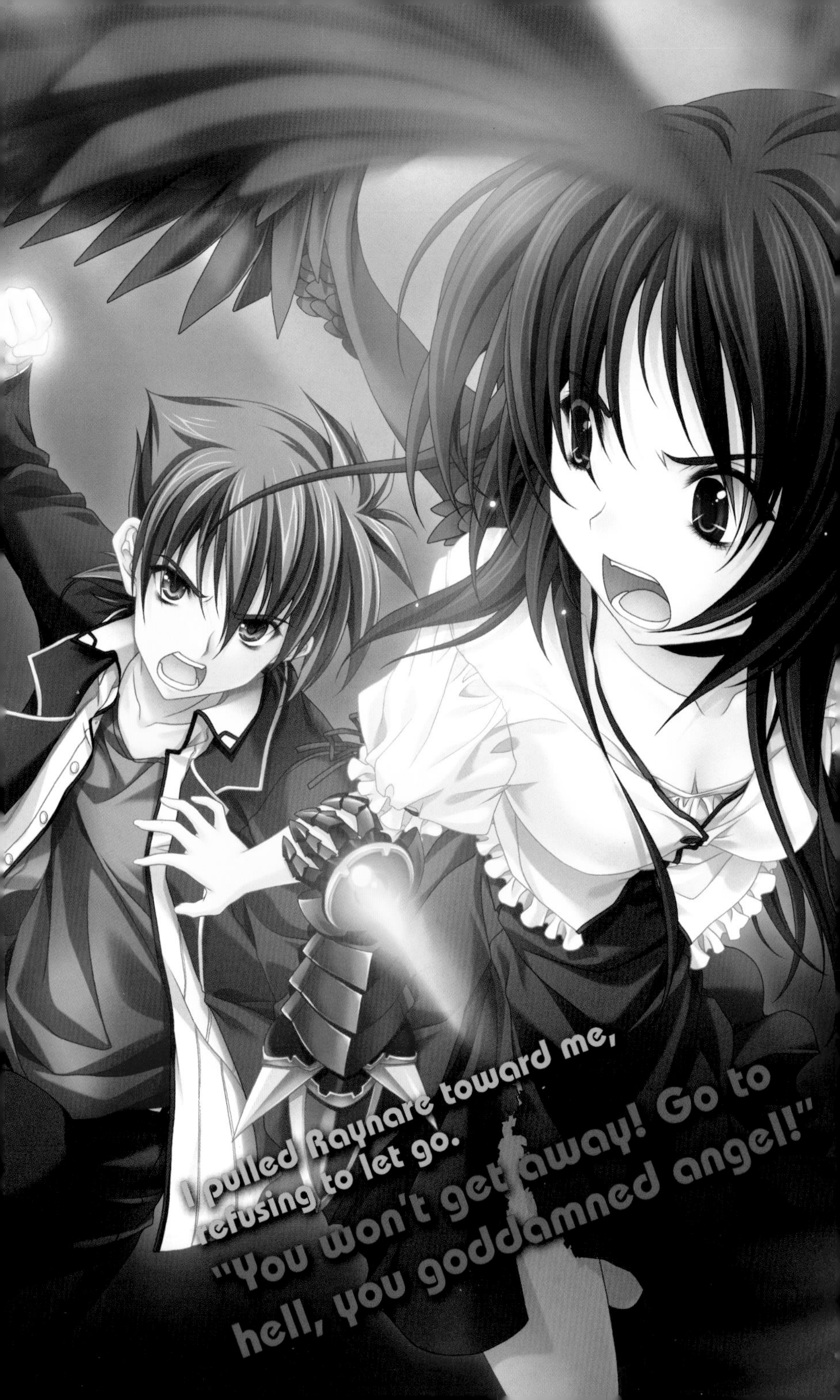
I pulled Raynare toward me, refusing to let go.
"You won't get away! Go to hell, you goddamned angel!"

DIABLOS OF THE OLD SCHOOL BUILDING

1

ICHIEI ISHIBUMI

ILLUSTRATION BY
MIYAMA-ZERO

YEN
ON

New York

Volume 1
Ichiei Ishibumi

Translation by Haydn Trowell
Cover art by Miyama-Zero

HIGH SCHOOL DxD Vol. 1 KYUKOSHA NO DIABOLOS
©Ichiei Ishibumi, Miyama-Zero 2008
First published in Japan in 2008 by KADOKAWA CORPORATION, Tokyo.
English translation rights arranged with KADOKAWA CORPORATION, Tokyo through TUTTLE-MORI AGENCY, INC., Tokyo.

English translation © 2020 by Yen Press, LLC

Yen On
150 West 30th Street, 19th Floor
New York, NY 10001

Visit us at yenpress.com
facebook.com/yenpress
twitter.com/yenpress
yenpress.tumblr.com
instagram.com/yenpress

First Yen On Edition: October 2020

Yen On is an imprint of Yen Press, LLC.
The Yen On name and logo are trademarks of Yen Press, LLC.

The publisher is not responsible for websites (or their content) that are not owned by the publisher.

Library of Congress Cataloging-in-Publication Data
Names: Ishibumi, Ichiei, 1981– author. | Miyama-Zero, illustrator. | Trowell, Haydn, translator.
Title: High school DxD / Ichiei Ishibumi ; illustration by Miyama-Zero ; translation by Haydn Trowell.
Other titles: Haisukūru Dī Dī. English
Description: First Yen On edition. | New York, NY : Yen On, 2020.
Identifiers: LCCN 2020032159 | ISBN 9781975312251 (v. 1 ; trade paperback)
Subjects: CYAC: Fantasy. | Demonology—Fiction. | Angels—Fiction. | High schools—Fiction. | Schools—Fiction.
Classification: LCC PZ7.1.I836 Hi 2020 | DDC [Fic]—dc23
LC record available at https://lccn.loc.gov/2020032159

ISBNs: 978-1-9753-1225-1 (paperback)
        978-1-9753-1226-8 (ebook)

10 9 8 7 6 5 4 3

LSC-C

Printed in the United States of America

CONTENTS

It's the same color as her hair.

As I stared at my bloodstained hand, that was all I could think of.
Red—a deeper, richer crimson than your usual strawberry-blond.
Yes, her long, beautiful, crimson hair was the same, brilliant color as
the blood now coating my hand.

Life.0

Issei Hyoudou—that's my name, but my friends and family just call me Issei. I'm in my second year of high school and enjoying the springtime of my youth.

I honestly can't say just how recognizable I am, but every now and then, someone will call out: "Hey, isn't that Issei?"

Maybe that's got you thinking I'm incredibly popular. I'm not. I have a reputation for lechery—so much so that I've even been accused of trying to peep into the changing room of the girl's kendo club.

I would never do anything so shameful...

Well, actually...I was there, in the storeroom next to the changing room. And I did try to catch a glimpse through a hole in the wall. I wasn't able to see anything, though. I mean, Matsuda and Motohama wouldn't get out of the damn way...

I had to put up with those two as they got themselves all worked up. "Whoa! Look at Murayama's breasts! They're huge!" one of them would exclaim while the other drooled, saying, "Katase sure has great legs..."

There's no way I didn't want to peep on that! Before I even had a chance, though, we heard footsteps approaching the storeroom, so we had to make our escape.

Then, seemingly out of nowhere, happiness came flying right into the arms of this perverted second-year.

"Will you go out with me?"

A confession from a girl! For a guy like me, who had never had a girlfriend before, it was a breath of fresh air. I was ready to taste the complicated flavors of adolescence.

My first ever girlfriend—Yuuma Amano, a slender girl with silky, jet-black hair. She was so cute. I fell head over heels in love with her at first sight. I mean, wouldn't you jump at the opportunity if an incredible beauty came running your way, calling out: *Hyoudou! I love you! Will you go out with me?*

Given my history with the opposite sex and how long I had been waiting to get a girlfriend, this situation was beyond my wildest dreams. You might think that sounds like a dating sim, but it really happened! It was a miracle! A beautiful young woman actually confessed her love to me!

Honestly, I thought it was a prank at first. I couldn't help but wonder whether Yuuma's friends had put her up to it, as revenge for something I'd done. They could've been hiding out of sight, watching us. Can you blame me? Up until that moment, I'd always believed I'd been born under some unlucky star, forever doomed to lack that certain appeal.

However, from that day on, I had a girlfriend! My world had changed. I don't know how to explain it, but I had found my place on this planet. I wanted to charge down the corridors, calling out *I've finally done it!* to everyone I passed.

I started pitying my girlfriend-less buddies, Matsuda and Motohama. That was just how generous of heart I had become.

So Yuuma and I became a couple, and the day of our first date quickly arrived. The time had come to put the plan I had laid out way back when into action.

Heh-heh, I must've brushed my teeth a dozen times the night before. There wasn't a speck of plaque left to be found. I even bought new underwear. You never know what might happen… My whole life had been in anticipation of this moment, after all!

I arrived at the meeting place three whole hours ahead of Yuuma and waited. To pass the time, I counted the number of girls in glasses who went by. Result: over one hundred!

After a while, some weirdo handed me a suspicious leaflet. YOUR WISHES GRANTED! it read, complete with an occult-looking magic circle.

…I wanted to throw it away but couldn't afford to leave our meeting place, so I stuffed it into my pocket.

At last, Yuuma finally arrived.

"Good timing. I just got here myself," I called to her. Bull's-eye! I'd always wanted to say that!

We held hands while we walked. The whole thing was pretty moving. I was on a date, strolling hand-in-hand with my gorgeous girlfriend! Really, I was so touched, I felt like I was going to break into tears. *Don't rush it,* I warned myself. This wasn't the time to get cocky.

From there, we made the most of our first date. Yuuma and I checked out a few clothing stores, had a look at some home decor—that sort of thing.

We had lunch together in a chain restaurant, just like your typical high school couple. Yuuma seemed to really enjoy her chocolate parfait. I was having my fill just watching her.

Ah, so this was how other teenagers felt when they went out on dates. *This* was living.

Mom, thanks for giving birth to me. Dad, I admit I was afraid I wouldn't be able to keep the family line going, but you don't have to worry about that anymore.

Before I knew it, one of the staff came to tell us it was getting late. I had almost reached the climax! A kiss?! A good-bye kiss?! So much blood was pumping into my head, I thought it might explode! Maybe I could even take this to the next level?!

Can you blame me for such thoughts? I'm a high schooler at the height of my budding sexuality!

At dusk, we went to a park on the outskirts of town. It wasn't a particularly popular area. There was no one there but us. Maybe that's

why my mind keep going to dirty places. Should I have better prepared myself by reading more erotic how-to guides? Before I could do
anything, Yuuma let go of my hand and walked up to the fountain.

"I had fun today," she said with a smile, the fountain behind her.

Whoa! She was already super-cute, but damn, with her back to the
sunset, it was almost like a movie or something.

"You know, Issei..."

"What is it, Yuuma?"

"I want to do something to commemorate our first date. Could you
do me a favor?"

This was it!

You know I was ready for *anything*! What else could she have been
talking about?! My breath—check! I was prepared! My heart was racing!

"Wh-what kind of favor...?" Ah, my voice was a little high. Yuuma
was going to know I was having dirty thoughts! I had come so far, only
to slip up in the most idiotic way imaginable... But Yuuma just smiled
back at me graciously.

Then, with her voice loud and clear, she said, "Could you die for me?"

....

...Huh? What?

"...Eh? You... Um, sorry, could you say that again? I think there's
something wrong with my ears." I *must* have misheard. Yes, I was mistaken, obviously. That's why I asked her to repeat herself.

And yet...

"Could you die for me?" Yuuma asked again, her innocent voice still
as clear as it had been a second ago.

It didn't make any sense. I forced a smile and was about to tell her
how funny a joke it was when...

Whoosh. A pair of huge, black wings burst out of Yuuma's back.
They beat back and forth violently, and a jet-black feather came flitting
through the air to land at my feet.

What on earth was going on? I mean, Yuuma might have been as
sweet as an angel, but this...

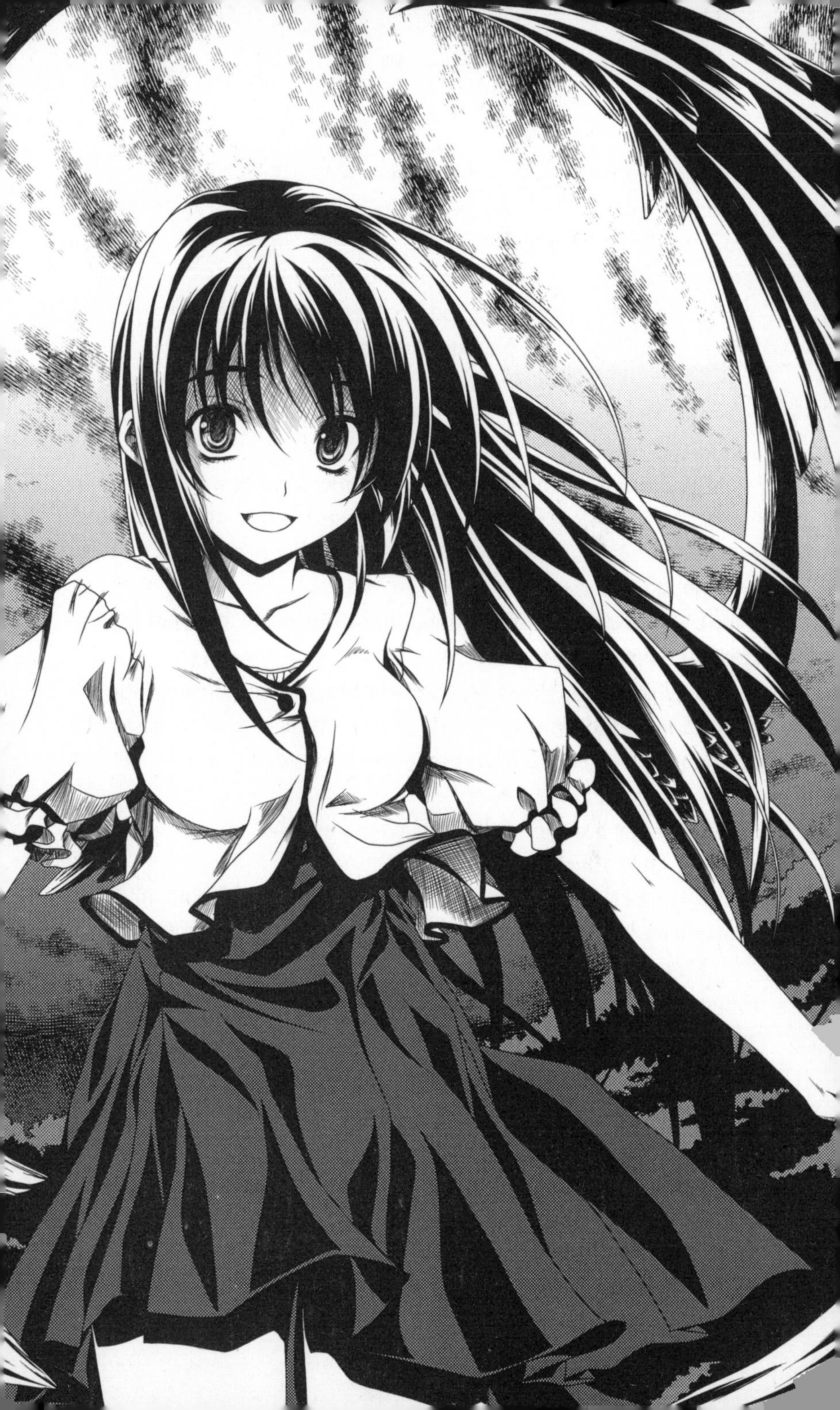

A real angel? No way. Was this some kind of act, then? My beautiful girlfriend now had black wings beating behind her. It was like something straight out of a fantasy.

But I didn't believe in that kind of thing.

Yuuma's cute, adorable eyes had become frighteningly cold.

"Although short-lived, playing innocent and lovey-dovey with you these past few days has been fun." Yuuma's tone was like ice, her rich voice now that of an adult. The corners of her mouth curled up in a faint smile.

A heavy sound shook the air. It was reminiscent of a game console booting up but deeper, weightier. It was so loud, my ears throbbed with a low ringing. That's when *it* appeared in her hands.

A long, slender spear.

Wait, was it glowing? The thing looked like it was *made* of light… That was no normal weapon.

Swoosh. There was the sound of something tearing through the air, followed by a dull *thwack*! At first, it just felt like something grazing my stomach, but Yuuma's weapon pierced me right through. She had thrown the spear at me…

Wait, hold on a second. Why? I tried to pull it out, but the blade disappeared into thin air.

All that was left was a gaping, bleeding hole in my abdomen. Blood surged from the wound.

My head was growing dizzy, my vision blurring. Before I realized it, my legs had given way, and I fell to the ground. Footsteps approached, one after another. Yuuma's faint voice reached my ears.

"Sorry. Your existence poses a threat to us, you see. We had to take care of you quickly. If you want to blame someone, blame God for giving you that Sacred Gear in the first place."

…Sacred…what…?

In my present state, I couldn't even form the words. The footsteps faded away into the distance. At the same time, I was starting to lose consciousness. The gaping hole in my stomach—it had to be fatal, but somehow, it didn't hurt.

Still, I knew I wasn't in a good way, given that I could literally feel myself slipping into unconsciousness. The temptation to crawl away and fall into a deep sleep was high, but if I did, I knew I would never wake up.

Seriously... I was only a second-year high school student. I wasn't ready to die. I hadn't even lived half my life yet!

This was pathetic! I was about to give up the ghost all because my girlfriend had stabbed me in some park!

Ugh... My consciousness was waning by the second. It felt like all these parts inside me were disappearing. I wondered what school was going to be like tomorrow.

Would Matsuda and Motohama be shocked by my death? Would they mourn for me? To think they might be the only ones who would care enough to shed a tear...

Mom, Dad... I won't be able to look after you in your old age...

This was no laughing matter... What would my parents think if they found all those erotic magazines I had hidden in my room after I was gone?

...Dammit, why was *that* all I could think about when I was on the brink of death...?

My hands... I could still move them. I reached down to my stomach, then lifted my hand back up in front of my face. Red... My blood. My whole hand was red with my blood. That's when I remembered her.

The image of a young woman floated up into my vision. She was a crimson-haired beauty. Every time I laid eyes on her, my gaze was inexplicably drawn to her brilliant hair. If I was going to die, why couldn't it have been in the arms of someone like her...?

I felt a pang of guilt, as if I was cheating on my girlfriend, Yuuma. Hold on—Yuuma was the one who'd practically signed my death warrant... If I really *was* gonna go, I wish it could have been after I'd had a chance to feel her up...

Ha, even my imminent death wasn't enough to put an end to my perverted fantasies...

Ah, everything was going dark...

Was this finally the end...?

Dammit, I had lived a pretty boring life...

...If I got the chance to be reborn, I would...

"Are you the one who called me?"

All of a sudden, a figure appeared before me. I couldn't tell who it was, what with how blurry my vision had become.

"You're dying. Your wound... Oh? Interesting. You must be... Yes, very interesting..."

Whoever it was began to chuckle, as if finding the whole situation rather amusing.

What exactly was so funny about this...?

"Seeing as you're about to die anyway, I'll take you for my own. From this moment onward, you will live your life for me."

The last thing I saw before I finally passed out was crimson hair.

Life.1
I'm Done Being Human!

"Wake up! Wake up! If you don't wake up, I'll…I'll…I'll kiss you…!"

"…Ngh."

The alarm clock spouted its typical tsundere line, but it wasn't sufficient to rouse its owner from his bed. He just tumbled out of a nightmare and flat onto the floor.

That guy was me, in case you hadn't realized.

…I hated waking up like that. I'd had that awful nightmare again. All my dreams recently had been about Yuuma killing me. Still, since I was clearly very much alive, they couldn't have been anything more than that.

"Wake up, Issei!" came Mom's usual summons from downstairs.

"All right, I'm coming!" I called back, rising from my spot on the floor.

Things were off to a bad start again today. For some reason, I'd been feeling so despondent lately. With a deep sigh, I started changing into my school uniform.

—○●○—

"I'm off," I said with a yawn as I left the house. I squinted at the bright, morning sun as I set off on the road to school, feeling listless.

Lately, being out in the sun had been making me feel drained and weak. The rays seemed to burn right through my skin. Anyway, morning light just didn't agree with me. I was not an early riser. That's why my mom kept hauling me out of bed every day. I was fine in the evenings, though. Better than fine, actually. Something inside me seemed to come alive after dusk. I had turned into a total night owl. It was weird.

It shouldn't have been like this. Sure, I stayed up late sometimes, but usually, it was a miracle if I could keep my eyes open past one o'clock in the morning. These days, I had no problem staying awake past three or four. There were even times I'd waited until sunrise before nodding off.

It wasn't like I was hooked on online games or late-night TV or anything. Something was happening to my body…

Was my brain trying to keep me from falling asleep? Maybe it was to hold back those dreams where I kept getting killed? Even if that's how it felt, there was no way that was right. The human body needs sleep, after all.

That didn't stop the feeling from taking hold of me each night, though—it was completely different from anything I had ever experienced before. The sensation was difficult to explain, but it was like this really uneasy intensity that kept building up deep inside me.

I had gone out the night before to see if that made a difference. Weirdly, my feet felt like they'd become lighter, and my whole body looked as though it was melting away into the darkness. My heart positively shook with joy. I broke into a run for the hell of it and took off faster than even I could believe.

If I join the track-and-field team, they'd probably make me a starter without a second thought. I was filled with enough energy to run a full marathon without breaking a sweat.

Maybe I let it get to my head a little, but when I tried to do the same thing during the day, my stamina was so poor, it made the previous night feel like a lie. I mean, it was still pretty average for a high schooler, but it was nothing compared with how I was after dark.

Yep, something strange came over me at night.

This probably sounds like the kind of thing a crazy person might say, but whatever—this sensation of release and excitement gave me the sense that I'd morphed into a completely different person.

Ugh... The morning sunshine really was grueling, though. In contrast to how I got at night, mornings were incredibly trying. No matter how you looked at it, there was definitely something wrong with me. More than anything, I couldn't shake the idea that something about me had changed the day I went out with Yuuma.

Kuou Academy—that's the private school I go to.

These days, it's coed, but up until a few years back, it had been an all-girls high school, so there were still more girls than boys. The ratio was closer to an even split in the lower grades, but the girls outnumbered the guys overall.

Even in my second-year class, the female-to-male ratio was seven to three, and it went to eight-to-two for third-years. Girls still dominated school life. There were more of them on the student council, including its president. It was the kind of school culture where boys were kind of limited in what they could do, but that hadn't stop me from choosing to attend.

My reasoning was simple enough. The place just had too many lovely ladies. It was wonderful! Yes, it was all thanks to my perverted nature that I'd been able to pass the infamously arduous entrance exams for Kuou Academy. I had wanted to take my classes surrounded by girls. That's the entire reason I picked this place.

Is there something wrong with that? What's wrong with being a pervert?! It's my life! I won't let anyone tell me otherwise! I'm going to make this school my harem! At least, that was my goal when I enrolled.

I felt pretty empty about the whole thing now, though. How foolish I was to think I could pick up two or three girlfriends here without even lifting a finger. Only the lady-killers, the real cool guys, had any luck. Girls wouldn't even look at me. They ignored me as if I were a piece of trash lying in the corridor.

Dammit! I hadn't taken any of that into account!

I was an idiot! If all had gone well, I should have been able to get my first girlfriend in no time! Then I could've broken up with her and met someone else, rinse and repeat for three years, and by the time graduation came around, I could have had them all fighting over me in an epic battle royal!

At the rate I was going, my dream would end up being nothing but a wild delusion! Maybe I was already deluding myself?

Where had I gone wrong?! Was I born in the wrong era? Had the tides of politics turned against me? Could it be...? Did the problem lie with me specifically?

Aaaaargh! I didn't even want to think about it! I was at my wit's end here. Sighing, I strolled into the classroom and took my seat.

"Yo, my brother-in-arms. How was that DVD I lent you? *Titillating*, am I right?"

The guy calling out to me was my friend, Matsuda. His close-cropped hair made him look like your typical sports guy, but he would come at you with all these lecherous comments that bordered on sexual harassment on an almost daily basis.

Matsuda had broken all kinds of athletic records back in middle school, but now he belonged to the photography club. He didn't bother hiding his intention to catch each girl in our school on film from every angle imaginable. It was for that reason that people had taken to calling Matsuda the Perverted Baldy or the Paparazzo of Sexual Harassment.

"Phew... The wind sure was strong this morning, huh? You wouldn't guess how many pairs of panties I managed to catch good views of."

The guy with glasses trying to act cool was my other friend, Motohama. He had this special ability he called "Scouter" that let him size up a girl's measurements with nothing more than those specs of his.

When he took them off, though, his power level plummeted. This had earned him the nicknames Perverted Glasses and Three-Size Scouter.

Matsuda and Motohama were my two partners in crime. I'm not joking when I say that seeing these two first thing in the morning really made me depressed.

"I've got some good stuff here," Matsuda said as he opened his bag and tipped its contents out on his desk without a hint of shame.

The books and DVDs piled up in front of him all had lewd and suggestive titles.

"Eek!"

One of the girls across the room let out a shriek. I couldn't really blame her. I mean, it was still first thing in the morning. Murmurs of "They're the worst!" and "Filthy perverts!" filled the room.

"Quiet! Who are you to deny us our worldly pleasures?! Look away, young ladies! Or I'll imagine myself having my way with you all!" Matsuda had no issue saying crude stuff like that.

Not too long ago, my eyes would have lit up at this sight, and I'd have asked where my friends had found such treasures. Now that my mornings had gotten so rough, though, I just couldn't get in the mood.

Matsuda let out a resigned sigh at my lethargic reaction. "Hey, come on. Why are you scowling like that when I've brought you all these goodies?"

"You've been really downbeat lately. Odd. Very odd. This isn't like you," Motohama said with obvious tedium as he adjusted his glasses.

"I *wish* I could get worked up over this. I'd like nothing more than to obsess over them. I'm just so drained right now."

"Are you sick? Nah, that can't be right. There's no way you, the human personification of desire itself, would let something like a cold get in your way."

I clenched my teeth in irritation at Motohama's offhand comment. At that moment, Matsuda slammed his fist into his hand, as if in sudden realization.

"Ah, I get it. This must be because of that imaginary girlfriend of yours. Yuuma, right?"

"…Come on, you're telling me you don't remember her?"

Matsuda and Motohama just stared back at me with pity in their eyes.

"Like we said, we've never heard of her. Seriously, you should get yourself checked out. Right, Motohama?"

"Yeah. I don't know how many times we've said this, but we've never even met this Yuuma girl you keep going on about."

…That's what they always said whenever I mentioned her. At first, I thought they were just messing with me. After having a serious conversation with them about it, though, I realized that wasn't the case.

I had definitely introduced Yuuma to both of them. I know because Matsuda and Motohama had come out the gate with rude comments the second they saw her. They'd said things like *"How come Issei's managed to get such a gorgeous girlfriend?!"* and *"This runs against the natural order of things… Issei, you didn't do anything illegal, did you?"*

In response, I haughtily suggested they should go find their own girlfriends. I remembered it like it was yesterday, but they didn't. My friends couldn't even recall who Yuuma was. It was as if she'd never even existed.

All that time I'd spent with her had seemingly disappeared, too. That was why my friends kept calling her imaginary. Though hard to accept, it was true that Yuuma's number and e-mail address weren't saved on my phone anymore.

Had someone deleted them? But how? *I* certainly hadn't deleted them, so who had? I tried calling her number as best as I could remember it, but it was inactive. Did that mean she hadn't actually existed? Was it all in my head? That was absurd, and yet…

As much as I wanted to deny it, apart from my own memories, there was no evidence Yuuma had ever been real. Mulling it over, I realized I didn't even know her address. She was from another school, so I worked out where based on her uniform and started asking around.

No one knew anything about her there, either. Yuuma simply didn't exist. Just who had I been dating? Was it all a dream? Some fantasy I'd conjured up out of thin air? Had I just been boasting to Matsuda and Motohama about my fictional delusions all along?

…Come on now, I wasn't crazy, right? After all, I could remember her face so clearly. Things just didn't add up. It was like that strange energy that welled up inside me at night; something was definitely wrong.

I had sunken deep into my own doubts when Matsuda laid a hand on my shoulder. "Well, we *are* in the springtime of our youth, so these things happen. You guys should come over to my place after school. We can watch my secret collection together."

"A wonderful idea! Matsuda, you *must* invite our good friend Issei here, too!"

"Of course, my dear Motohama. We're all driven by the same lustful appetites. It would be an affront to our families if we failed to deliver on them."

The two of them broke out into lecherous guffaws. No matter how you looked at it, my friends were perverts all right, the both of them. I guess that made me one, too. Well, whatever. I had no trouble living as a deviant.

"All right! Today, there's no holding back! We'll toast with sodas, eat some snacks, and have our fill of erotic DVDs!" At a total loss, I resigned myself to going along with the proposal.

"Yeah, now we're talking! That's our Issei!"

"That's the spirit. Youth is to be savored, am I right?"

Matsuda and Motohama were certainly getting worked up. I just figured I'd put the whole thing with Yuuma on hold for a while. Taking breaks is important, you know! I was happy to forget about everything that had been going on and enjoy myself like a guy my age was supposed to!

Then, after we had made our plans for that afternoon, it happened. That brilliant crimson appeared before me yet again.

My eyes were fixed to the young woman strolling through the

schoolyard outside the classroom window. It was the crimson-haired beauty, the school idol whose features transcended human flesh. Her slim proportions weren't those of a typical Japanese girl.

That was to be expected. She wasn't Japanese, after all. She was from somewhere in northern Europe, apparently. Based on what I'd heard, she was attending school in Japan because of her father's job. There wasn't a soul at the academy who hadn't found themselves enchanted by her exquisite beauty.

Rias Gremory. She was a third-year student, which made her my senior.

When I took a look around, I realized the whole class was staring at her, Matsuda and Motohama included.

Something like this was pretty regular. Rias caught everyone's attention when she walked by. Some came to a complete halt, and others fell silent, but everyone found themselves turning to watch her. The wind blew gently through Rias's crimson hair as the entire student body watched.

Those radiant locks reached down to her waist, and with the breeze fanning it out behind her, it was as if Rias was walking against a scarlet backdrop. Her skin, white as snow, was stunning. *Beautiful* really was the only word to describe her.

Rias's overall allure and noble bearing were nothing short of mesmerizing. Whenever I saw her, I'd get so caught up in her elegant looks that I'd forget what I was doing. Lately, however, I'd started seeing her in a different light.

Yes, she was certainly beautiful, but almost *too* beautiful. In some deep corner of my heart, some part of me had grown wary of Rias's stunning figure. I couldn't explain why, but I was sure it had something to do with Yuuma's disappearance. At that very moment, Rias turned and locked her clear-blue eyes right on me.

—!

In that brief instant, it was though Rias had grabbed ahold of my very soul. What was this feeling? It was like going up against an opponent who held an overwhelming advantage. Rias narrowed her brilliant-blue eyes and curled her lips in a faint smile.

Was that for me? Don't be absurd, I thought. We had never even spoken to each other. But then I recalled something from that dream I kept having. At the end of that recurring vision, there was always a crimson-haired figure calling out to me. The voice had been a kind but, at the same time, impenetrably cold. However, before I had a chance to compare Rias with the vague image in my dreams, the girl disappeared.

"Gimme some tits to squeeze!" Matsuda wailed. I leaned over to comfort him as we finished the last film of our erotic DVD marathon.

Arriving at Matsuda's place after school, we happily began feasting on those forbidden delights. However, as the disks started piling up, our excitement cooled. My friends and I started asking ourselves why we were still single. The only thing that did was make us feel miserable; Matsuda had been crying nonstop for three whole videos now.

Motohama was pretending to keep his cool, but he couldn't hide the tears welling up behind his glasses. Half an hour earlier, Motohama had murmured under his breath: "You know, a while back, a girl asked me to meet her behind the school gym... That was the first time I'd ever been mugged..."

Even I felt like shedding tears hearing such an awful tale. Why on earth were the three of us getting so depressed watching a bunch of dirty videos?

No, I know the reason.

It was because we were so unpopular. Dammit. Knowing there were guys my age making passionate love to girls right this very moment filled me with hate for the injustices of the world. As those dark thoughts swirled about in my mind, the last film came to an end. The sun had long since set.

When I glanced at my watch, I realized it was already ten o'clock. I'd told my parents I was going to Matsuda's place, but they were bound to worry if I didn't get home soon. It was a school night, after all.

"Well, I'd better head off," I said. With that, we all rose to our feet and got ready to part ways.

"See ya," Motohama and I said in unison as we took off.

"What a nice evening. A good night for watching more erotic DVDs..." Motohama sighed heavily as he stared up at the open sky. He must have been feeling pretty down. Regardless, I trusted that he and Matsuda would no doubt return to their usual selves by morning.

"See you tomorrow, then."

"Yeah. Pleasant dreams, eh?" We parted ways, but Motohama seemed lifeless and sapped as he waved good-bye.

Maybe I'll send him a text later to see how he's doing.

A few minutes later, on the road home, my newfound nocturnal vigor began to surge. That strange nighttime force had struck again.

Yep, there was definitely something wrong with me. There was no way this could be normal. My eyes sharpened, and my senses were more finely attuned to my surroundings. My vision and hearing grew so sensitive that I could see clearly through the dark of night and even make out conversations going on in nearby houses.

Seriously! Being able to see down unlit streets with no problem is weird, right? I felt like whatever was happening to me was getting stronger by the day.

This was definitely more than my imagination. I mean, the chills coursing through my body were the real deal!

I had felt someone watching me for a while now. Some cold gaze had locked onto me. A foreboding aura hung over the path ahead. My body was trembling more and more by the second.

The source of my discomfort was a man dressed in a suit who was staring at me. It was closer to sneering, actually. If I had met his gaze head-on, I probably would've been too scared to move. I'd heard people talk about stuff like *murder in the eyes* before, but was this what they meant?

I could definitely feel his hostility. No, it was more dangerous than that. This suit bastard was out to hurt me! The man stepped toward me, silent and sure. There was no mistaking it; he was coming right for me!

Is he a slasher?! Something worse?! This is bad! Seriously, I couldn't stop shaking! Why did I have to come paths with some psycho on my way home?!

"What checkered luck to meet one like you in a no-name town like this."

………?

Huh? What is he talking about? No, it's irrational to expect a psycho-path to make any sense. Yeah, it was pretty safe to say I was in trouble! What was I going to do if he pulled out a knife or something?! I didn't know any kind of self-defense. I'd never even been in a fight before!

That's when I remembered that my strength powered up at night! That was it! I could make my escape! Taking a step backward, I tried to put some distance between us, but the menacing figure in the suit began quickly closing the gap.

"Trying to turn tail? Who is your master? Must be low-ranked to choose a place like this. What's their game? Tell me, who is it?"

I didn't have the faintest idea what the hell he was even talking about! With a sudden lurch, I took off at full speed, heading back the way I had come. I was fast, insanely fast. This might sound like a weird thing to say about yourself, but my legs were downright superhuman.

I tore through the darkness, turning down one unfamiliar street after the next. Strangely, I wasn't out of breath. That being the case, I decided to keep going until I was sure the suit guy wouldn't be able to follow. After about fifteen minutes, I found myself in a wide-open area: a park.

I slowed my pace to a normal walking speed and approached the nearby fountain to take a short rest. Glancing around, a curious thought caught me as I stood in the pale illumination of the streetlights.

I know this place...

This was the spot from my dreams—the place I went with Yuuma at the end of our date! I really needed to get ahold of myself. Was this a coincidence? A miracle? Had I brought myself here subconsciously? No way.

A deathly chill shot down my spine. There was someone behind me... I could feel it.

I turned around slowly, and a jet-black feather fluttered down in front me. Was it a crow?

"Did you think you could escape? You inferior creatures can be such pests." The suited prick from before was back, this time with huge black wings sprouting out of his back.

Was this guy an angel? No, they only existed in fairy tales, right? Was he cosplaying, then? But those wings looked too real for that. Did that mean they were actually real? I just couldn't bring myself to accept that!

"Give me the name of your master. Your kind are a nuisance, especially in a place like this. As far as we're concerned... Wait, don't tell me you're a stray? If you're without a master, then explain what you're doing here." The weird psychopath kept mumbling one thing after another.

Nutjobs like this guy need to quit convincing themselves of their own delusions!

This was a worrying development, but I quickly found myself remembering the incident from my dreams. At the very end of that date, Yuuma killed me in front of this exact fountain in this exact park. Back then, she'd had black wings sprouting from her back, too. Now this guy had shown up with the same black wings... Had it been a premonition?

Why did such a cute girl have to be replaced by a guy?!

Wait, that wasn't important! What mattered was that things were going downhill for me, fast! If events now were playing out like in the dream, the next thing to happen would be…

"Hmph. I sense neither your master nor your brethren. No one trying to hide their presence. No magic circles. Given the circumstances, you *must* be a stray. In that case, there's no one to stop me from killing you." The man spoke ominously as he held out his hand.

Whatever the freak was talking about, he was motioning toward me! A dull sound rang in my ears. I knew what would happen next. Light seemed to gather around the winged man's hand. It was bad enough having to put up with this fantasy stuff in my dreams, but out here in the waking world, too?!

The light bulged and stretched into the form of a spear, just like I knew it would. This was what had happened in the dream, and *that* definitely hadn't ended well! This man was going to kill me! Before I could even finish thinking, the spear had pierced my stomach, and a strange sensation was welling up inside me.

Cough!

Blood spurted out my mouth, followed by a shrieking pain.

Damn, this hurts! I collapsed to my knees. My insides felt like they were burning. The horrible sensation was spreading throughout my body, and it was too much to bear. Even a word like *agony* didn't do it justice.

I tried pulling the spear out, but the second I touched it, pain coursed through my hand. The weapon was hot, hot enough to leave my hand burned and scorched.

"Guh… Ugh…," I moaned, tortured. It just hurt too much!

Given what that spear made of light had done to my hand, was it burning me inside, too? Just the thought seemed to intensify the pain. Was this what it felt like to be cooked from the inside out? Tears of anguish coursed down my cheeks.

Footsteps approached, one after another. Above me, the man was gathering light to form another spear.

"That must be painful. Light is poison to your kind, after all. The damage it inflicts isn't something you can just shrug off. Here I was thinking that a middling spear would be enough to finish you, but you're tougher than I thought. Let's try again, then, shall we? But this time, how about I put a little more light into it? Prepare yourself."

This was it—the finishing blow. Another hit like that, and I'd be done for! It was that thought that took me back to my recurring dream.

Crimson. That brilliant crimson...

No. There was no way she would help me. That part was only in the dream. Still, all this matched what had happened in that vision so clearly. Maybe this was a dream, too?

If this is all some nightmare, then someone should be coming to help by now! I don't want to die like this, even if it isn't real!

Swoosh.

There was an earsplitting gust of wind, and the air in front of me suddenly exploded. When I looked up, the man's fingers were smoldering. Blood was dripping from his arm.

"I'll ask you to keep your hands off him."

A tall, feminine figure sauntered past me. *That crimson hair.* Even from behind, I could tell who she was: the person from my dream. I had never been able to make out her face before, but I knew this was her.

"...Crimson hair... You must be from the House of Gremory..." The man glared at my savior, his eyes burning with hatred.

"Rias Gremory. Pleased to meet you, my dear fallen angel. I warn you, I shall show no mercy if you lay a hand on him."

Rias Gremory. Right, that was the name of the crimson-haired beauty, that third-year from school.

"...Heh. What're you saying? This creature belongs to you? Who would have guessed this is your territory? Well then, allow me to apologize for this little misunderstanding. I warn you, however, not to let your servants run loose. They might bump into someone like me."

"I appreciate the friendly advice. Bear in mind, this town is under my watch. If anything like this happens again, I won't hold back."

"Let me return the same admonition to you, heir apparent of the esteemed House of Gremory. My name is Dohnaseek. It would be best if we did not cross paths again."

The man spread his black wings and floated into the air. He gave Rias and I one final scowl from above before disappearing into the night. Did this mean the danger had finally passed?

I felt a touch of relief, but my vision was blurring. Staying conscious was growing more difficult every second. I guess you could say things still weren't going great for me.

"Oh, are you about to faint? That's certainly an ugly wound. Very well. Tell me, where do you—?" Rias crouched down beside me, but I wasn't able to catch the end of her sentence.

I had already slipped into oblivion.

—○●○—

"...*Wake up, or I'll kill you... Wake up, or I'll cut you to pieces...*"

It was morning when I awoke.

...*What's going on? Another nightmare?*

No way could it have been real, even if it had felt that way. Regardless, I was safe and sound in my bed now. Today, my alarm clock had woken me with a yandere-style voice. I guess it *had* been a dream after all.

This time, it hadn't been Yuuma who killed me but some guy. Both of them had black wings, though. I shook my head.

Pull yourself together! I told myself. Why did I keep waking up every morning after having the same vision?

The previous day, I'd gone to school, and nothing unusual had happened. Afterward, Motohama and I had stopped by Matsuda's place for an erotic DVD marathon. Then I'd headed home and, on the way, found myself attacked by some psycho with wings sprouting out his back...

My train of thought suddenly petered out as I realized the state I was in. To put it bluntly, I was naked. I wasn't even wearing any underwear! Totally commando! I couldn't remember a thing after that spear got me! How did I get home? Was I going senile already? No matter what had gone down, I wasn't the kind of guy who went to bed naked.

"...Ngh..."

—!

The sound of a silky, sensual voice caught my ear. I glanced timidly to my side.

"Zzz... Zzz..."

A crimson-haired beauty was sleeping soundly beside me...and she was just as naked as I was. Her snow-white skin was positively dazzling—so smooth and rich.

......

This was all too much. It was definitely her, the idol of my school. Her blood-red hair spread out over the pillow was nothing short of mesmerizing.

Rias Gremory was naked in bed with me.

......

Huh? Wait, seriously?! I tried to calm myself down by counting prime numbers. *Two, three, five, seven, eleven, thirteen, seventeen, nineteen, twenty-three...*

Argh! It was no good! I couldn't get ahold of myself! Why was I in bed with Rias? What the hell had happened last night? More importantly, what did I do?! I couldn't remember a thing!

I racked my brain trying to remember how it all could have happened. Had I slept with her?! Was this how I had lost my virginity?! Impossible! It couldn't be!

Remember! I told myself. *You've got to remember!*

What had I done? How did we end up like this? I was so confused, I felt like my head was on the verge of exploding. Little did I know, things were about to get worse.

"Issei! Get out of bed! It's time for school!"

"Honey, is he in his room?"

"His shoes are by the door, so he must have come home. Just what makes him think he can stay at his friend's so late? Now he won't make it to school on time! When I get my hands on him…!"

I could hear my parents talking downstairs. Then there were footsteps climbing up the staircase. They were angry and heavy, completely different from my mom's usual pace. She was on her way up!

Wait! Don't come in! If she saw me like this, there was no telling what she might do!

"Hold on! I'm getting up! I'm getting up, so don't—"

"I won't put up with this anymore! We're going to have a talk, young man!"

My mom was pissed all right, and she was coming in my room. She was gonna open the door. I couldn't let her see me like this!

"Ngh… Is it morning?"

—?!

Rias, still lying beside me, spoke as if she was still half-asleep. This was even worse. *Half-asleep* basically meant *awake*!

Click.

The door burst open—and at the very same moment, Rias sat up in bed. My eyes met my mom's. She was angry all right. Indignant.

"Good morning," Rias said, beaming.

My mom's gaze shifted from me to Rias. Her face was frozen. She glanced back at me, but I looked away.

"…*Get. Ready. Now,*" she seethed through gritted teeth before silently closing the door behind her.

A second later, my mother's furious footsteps thundered down the stairs.

"Ahhhhhhhhhhh! *Dear!*"

"What is it? You're fuming! Was Issei doing something lewd again?"

"Se-se-se-se-se-sex! Issei! With a foreignerrrr!"

"What?! Honey! What happened?!"

"In-in-international…! Issei was…!"

"Honey?! Calm down! Honey!"

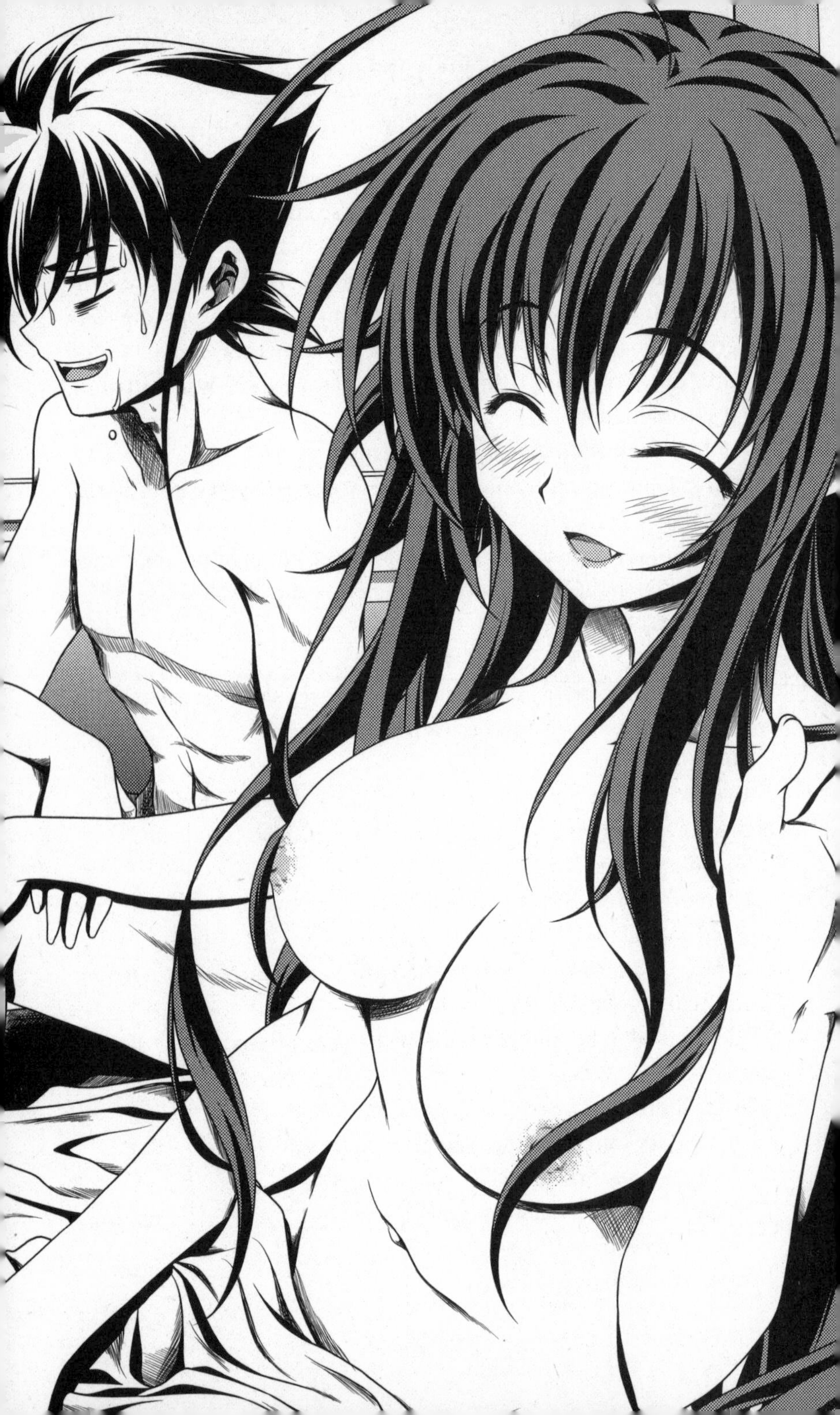

All I could do was bury my face in my hands. It was easy enough to imagine what was going on downstairs. How could this have happened? There was definitely going to be a family discussion now. No excuse would be able to explain this away!

"You have a lively family," Rias said as she nimbly rose from my bed and went to retrieve her uniform from my desk. She was naked. Beautifully naked. I—I could see everything…

Her narrow hips. Her long, shapely legs. Her thighs. Her nicely shaped buttocks. Not to mention her breasts, which were rich and voluptuous… Even her nipples! Did Rias have any plans of actually covering herself? Was she some kind of an exhibitionist?!

If I had been blessed with Motohama's Three-Size Scouter ability, I would have been able to ascertain her measurements then and there. Oh, how I wish I had his gift!

Nonetheless, I knew one thing for sure. I had seen a lot of naked women in erotic books and adult movies, but Rias put them all to shame. How do I describe it? She was like art, fashioned with meticulously honed style and technique. Rias was like one of those nude paintings in a fine-art textbook or a sculpture in a museum—sheer perfection. Words weren't enough. She was amazing.

Still…I was starting to feel awkward staring at her like this. I couldn't let her think I was a total pervert.

"R-Rias!" I stammered.

"What?"

"Y-your breasts…," I murmured, glancing away. "I can see them!" Of course, I wanted to keep looking, but I had to restrain myself.

"Go ahead," Rias replied boldly as she changed into her uniform with a benign smile.

—!

Can words even be used like that? A surge of electricity coursed through my flesh.

My eyes started welling with tears at the sound of that wonderful phrase. Such language was the kind you could never hear in school. I was touched, truly moved!

"How's your stomach?" Rias asked.

My stomach? I reached down to my abdomen while I watched the beautiful, red-haired girl getting dressed.

"You were stabbed yesterday."

—!

With that, I snapped back to attention. I recalled that some guy with black wings had stabbed me in the park last night, using a spear that looked like it was made of light. There was nothing wrong with my stomach now, though. I was sure the attack had gouged a huge hole right through me, and yet…there was no way a wound like that would've healed in such a short time. Not when there had been so much blood. Did that mean it had been a nightmare?

"Just so you know, it wasn't a dream," Rias said, as if reading my thoughts.

"It—it was pretty bad, though…"

"I healed you. It was a mortal wound, but you're tougher than you look. That, combined with my powers, is what saved you. I had to embrace you—naked—in order to use my magic to give you strength. Members of the same Familia can do that."

Whatever Rias was saying didn't make any sense to me.

Hold on. She said we embraced…naked?

…………

EHHHHHHHHHHHHHHHHHHHHH?!

So that must mean…!!!

"Don't worry. I'm still a virgin," Rias said, as if peering into my mind yet again.

Ah, of course. For some reason, that came as a relief. Hold on, *should* I have been so relieved?

"Don't look at me like that. The world is filled with more mystery than you could possibly imagine." Rias drew close, dressed only in her underwear, and stroked my cheek with her slender fingers.

My face unconsciously turned a bright red. Being fawned over like this by a half-naked beauty made it tough to do otherwise.

"My name is Rias Gremory," said the crimson-haired girl. "I'm a demon."

A demon? Is this a joke? She can't be serious. I had no idea what to make of it.

"I'm also your master now. Nice to meet you, Issei Hyoudou. Is just Issei all right?"

I didn't know what to make of her claim, but Rias's smile certainly looked demonic.

"Let's eat."

Grandfather, I know you're up there in Heaven. I need your help.

By my side, in my own house, a beautiful young woman was sipping at a bowl of miso soup.

"This is delicious, Mother."

"A-ah… Y-you're welcome."

My parents were sitting across the table with complicated expressions too intense to describe.

Grandfather, what's going on here? What am I supposed to do?

Breakfast had never been this awkward before. I was straining my brain trying to figure out what I was supposed to do.

"Issei, your mother went out of her way to make this. Now eat up," Rias ordered calmly, almost as if she were my older sister.

"Y-yes!" I replied hastily and hurriedly started wolfing down my own food.

"Don't be so ill-mannered. Eat slowly so you can savor the taste. There's no substitute for your own mother's home cooking," Rias scolded, wiping at the corners of her mouth with a handkerchief.

What exactly *was* this situation?

"I-Issei…," my dad began timidly. He was trembling, but I probably was, too. "Wh-who is this young lady?"

At this question, Rias put down her chopsticks and bowed her head. "…I apologize for not having introduced myself. That was terribly rude of me. I've brought shame to the House of Gremory. Please allow me to start over. Father, Mother, my name is Rias Gremory. I attend Kuou Academy with your son. It's a pleasure to meet you both." The crimson-haired girl flashed my parents an elegant smile.

"I—I see… Oh my, ha-ha! Are you from overseas? Your Japanese is excellent."

"Yes. I've been living in Japan for a long time due to my father's work."

It looked like Rias's answer had satisfied my dad. My mom, however, didn't look so convinced.

"Rias… Can I call you that?"

"Of course, Mother."

"Just what kind of relationship do you have with Issei?"

—!

What a simple, unadorned way of asking about the situation she'd found Rias and I in this morning. My mom leaned forward suspiciously, but Rias simply smiled back at her sweetly.

"We're just high school classmates who get along well, Mother."

"That's a lie!" my mom countered immediately.

Her reaction was understandable. That kind of excuse wouldn't work. Not after what she had seen.

"I m-m-m-mean… You were both…! In bed…!"

"Issei said he has been having nightmares, so I offered to sleep next to him."

"Next to him?! B-but you were naked! Both of you!"

"Yes, that's how young people sleep these days, Mother."

That's one hell of a lie, Rias. However, it seemed to have worked, as my mom fell silent.

"I—I see…," she stammered after a moment. "So that's how young people sleep these days?"

Mom?! Are you going to accept that?! Really?! Then I noticed something strange about my mom's eyes. They were hollow, empty, as if she'd been possessed by something.

Rias turned and whispered in my ear, "I'm sorry. It looked like she might cause a fuss, so I used my abilities on her."

Her abilities? Only then did I remember that Rias had introduced herself as a demon a short while ago. Is that what she meant by "abilities"?

Rias turned back to her breakfast. When I looked closely, my dad's eyes were just as hollow as my mom's. Had she used her power on him, too?

A demon… What exactly was going on here?

Everyone kept staring at me on my way to school the next morning, and I could understand why. After all, Rias Gremory, the idol of our school, was walking beside me, and I was carrying her bag, as if I were her manservant.

"Why is *he* doing that…?"

"What is Rias doing with a creep like him…?"

From every direction, boys and girls alike cried out in bewilderment. Some even fainted from shock.

What's so wrong with this, huh? Is it really so bad for Rias to interact with me?!

Rias and I strode through the school's front gate, and at the entrance to the main building, we parted ways.

"I will send someone for you later. We have business after school," Rias declared with a soft smile.

Send someone? What's that supposed to mean? Still unsure what was going on, I headed for my classroom. The second I opened the door, all eyes locked on me. It wasn't too surprising. I had been seen with Rias, after all.

Whack!

Someone hit me on the back of the head. When I turned around, I found Matsuda waiting for me and Motohama beside him.

"What's all this?!" Matsuda shrieked with tears in his eyes. From his expression alone, I could guess what he was about to say next. "We were supposed to be hard-luck brothers!"

"Issei, explain yourself. What happened after we parted ways last night?" Motohama, unlike Matsuda, was trying to act calm as he adjusted his glasses, but his eyes looked as sharp as razors. Both of them were frightening in their own ways.

That didn't stop me from breaking out into a haughty laugh, however. Boldly, I asked, "Have you guys ever seen real breasts before?"

My words were enough to send shivers down their spines.

—○●○—

After school, a male student with half-open eyes came around asking about me. This was none other than the academy's number one most popular guy, Yuuto Kiba. That winning grin of his had pierced the heart of every girl in the school. He was actually in the same grade as me, although in a different class. Cries of excitement and joy sounded from every room as he walked down the hall. Damn, I hated that guy.

"So what do you want?" I asked dismissively.

Kiba's smile, however, didn't waver. "I've come on Rias Gremory's instructions."

—!

That one sentence was enough to tell me all I needed to know. This was who Rias had sent for me?

"…All right, I get it. So what do you want me to do?"

"Come with me."

"*Yaaaaah!*" The girls around me broke out into frenzied screams.

"Wh-what is Kiba doing with Hyoudou?!"

"He'll corrupt you, Kiba!"

"Unforgivable! A Kiba/Hyoudou pairing?!"

"Maybe it's more like Hyoudou/Kiba?!"

They were saying all kinds of crazy nonsense. *Damn, this is annoying.*

"All right," I nodded.

I'm going to put this out there: I hate popular guys. Still, I followed Kiba.

"H-hey, Issei!" Matsuda called out after me.

"Don't worry, bud. I'm not about to get into a fight or anything," I answered, trying to assure him there was nothing to be concerned about.

"What do you want me to do with *Me, the Groper, and the Occasional Udon*?!" Matsuda shouted, lifting an erotic DVD into the air.

I cried out to the heavens for someone to save me from this horrible situation.

I followed Kiba all the way to the other side of the school grounds, behind the main building, to a spot hidden behind some trees. It was the old school building, which was seemingly deserted.

The place had been in use a long time ago, but these days, there was no sign of activity whatsoever. Over time, the building had acquired an eerie, ominous reputation as one of the Seven Wonders of the academy.

Anyway, though old and built entirely from wood, the windows were all intact, and nothing actually looked damaged. All things considered, it wasn't that bad.

"The president is waiting for you," Kiba said.

The president? He must be talking about Rias. "President," huh? Does she belong to a club? I guess this means Kiba is a member, too, then?

My questions just kept piling up. Anyway, so long as I kept tagging along, Kiba was bound to take me to her. We went inside and climbed the staircase to the second floor, traveling deep into the building. The halls were clean, and even the unused rooms looked completely free of dust. There were none of the usual hallmarks of abandoned buildings.

No spiderwebs stretched across the ceiling, and no weeds sprouted from the floorboards. Someone must have been keeping the place tidy.

While I was ruminating over these observations, Kiba stopped in front of one of the classrooms. Apparently, we had reached our destination. I was surprised to find a nameplate hanging on the door to which Kiba had led me.

The words *Occult Research Club* were written on it.

The Occult Research Club? The name alone made me tilt my head in curiosity. It wasn't the existence of such a club that had me thinking but, rather, the idea that Rias Gremory was affiliated with such an odd extracurricular. "President, I've brought him," Kiba announced from outside the door.

"All right, come in," came Rias's response.

So she really is here, I thought.

As Kiba opened the door and we stepped inside, I was astonished by what lay before me.

Every square inch of the room seemed to be filled with strange symbols and glyphs. The floor, the walls, the ceiling—they were all covered with incomprehensible writing. At the center of it all was a magic circle. The complex pattern was huge, taking up almost the entire room. Just looking at it made my hair stand on end.

Apart from that, there were also a few sofas and some desks. Someone was sitting on one of the sofas—a short, diminutive girl...

I knew her. I'd seen her before. She was a first-year named Koneko Toujou! She might have been a high schooler like the rest of us, but with her childish face and petite build, she looked more like she belonged in elementary school.

Koneko was quite popular with some of the guys in school and even among the girls. She was like a living, adorable mascot. Koneko was nibbling silently at a *youkan*, a thick jellied sweet. She had the same drowsy look she wore every other time I'd seen her.

The girl was quite renowned for being incredibly stoic and expressionless. Kiba and I must have caught her attention, as she looked over at me.

"This is Issei Hyoudou," Kiba introduced.

Koneko Toujou bobbed her head. "Ah, hi."

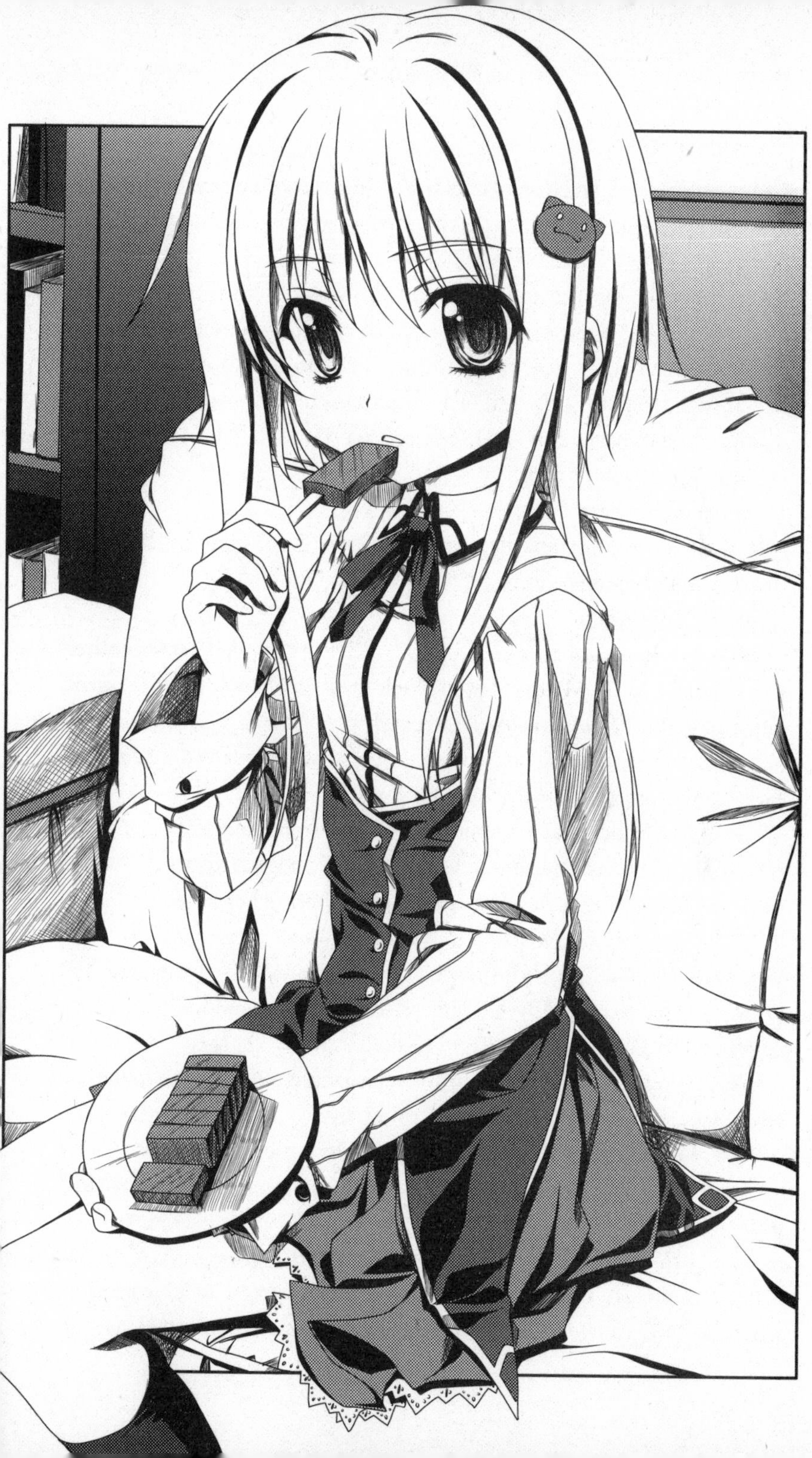

I bowed back in greeting. Koneko continued nibbling on her *youkan* in silence. Yep, just as I'd heard, she wasn't particularly chatty.

Splash!

I could make out the sound of running water from the back of the room. A shower, perhaps? When I looked carefully, I noticed a plastic curtain on the other side of the room. Through it, I spotted a silhouette. It was unmistakably that of a woman taking a shower.

Hold on, a shower? This room has a shower?!

Click. The sound of running water died away.

"Here you go, President."

Is there more than one person back there? I wondered. The voice clearly didn't belong to Rias.

"Thank you, Akeno."

From the sound of things, Rias was getting changed on the other side of the curtain. My mind went back to what I had seen this morning, and I could feel my face turning red.

You have a marvelous body, Rias. I guess I won't be needing to push my imagination particularly hard for a while.

"…What a lecherous expression," someone muttered.

When I turned to the source of the voice, I spotted Koneko Toujou. All I saw, though, was the same petite girl nibbling her *youkan*.

So I have a lecherous face, do I? Well, excuse me.

Whish! The curtain slid open to reveal Rias standing there in her uniform. Her dripping-wet, crimson hair made her look extremely alluring. She glanced my way and flashed a smile.

"My apologies. I wasn't able to wash last night since I was staying at your place, so I took a moment to freshen up."

Ah right. Still, the thing that really bothered me was that this room had a shower. My gaze shifted to the feminine figure standing behind Rias…

Wait, seriously?! My mouth fell wide open in surprise.

A black ponytail! The ponytail was an endangered species around where I lived! It was said only one such creature remained at our school. That gentle face with an everlasting smile. That exquisitely classic Japanese bearing. That paragon of feminine virtue! She was yet another of my school's most famous stars, Akeno Himejima!

She and Rias were colloquially known as the Two Great Ladies! They commanded the admiration of men and women alike!

"Oh dear. Greetings, I'm Akeno Himejima. Pleased to make your acquaintance," she said with a polite expression. Her voice was absolutely enthralling.

"S-same here. Issei Hyoudou. N-nice to meet you!" I replied, my heart pounding.

Rias nodded to everyone. "It looks like we're all here now. Hyoudou—no, Issei…"

"Y-yes?"

"We, the Occult Research Club, welcome you…"

"Ah, er, thanks."

"…as a demon."

—!

Mom, Dad—I get the feeling I'm in for something big.

"Some tea."

"Ah, thanks."

Akeno Himejima brought a cup of tea over to the sofa where I was sitting. I sipped at the warm drink.

"It's good."

"Oh my, thank you." Himejima chuckled happily.

Kiba, Koneko Toujou, Rias, and I were all sitting on couches arranged around a table.

"Akeno, sit with us."

"Yes, President," Himejima replied, taking a seat next to Rias.

Everyone fixed their eyes on me. *Wh-what is it…?* I was starting to feel nervous with them all staring at me like that. Rias was the one who broke the silence.

"Allow me to put this simply. We're all demons."

…W-well, that was certainly *one way* to break the ice.

"You look like you don't believe me. Well, I can't blame you. You remember the man from last night, don't you? With the black wings?"

How could I forget? If it wasn't been a dream, then what I saw must have been real.

"He's a fallen angel—a being who used to serve Heaven but was sent to Hell as punishment for his evil deeds and intentions. His kind are our enemies."

Fallen angels, huh? It sounded like a fantasy video game.

"We demons have been at war with the fallen angels since time immemorial, fighting for hegemony over the underworld that humankind calls Hell. Each of the two factions controls one portion of the underworld. Demons like us build our strength by forging pacts with humans and exacting payment. Fallen angels seek to manipulate humanity and destroy demons. There are also proper angels, who follow the will of Heaven, indiscriminately targeting demons and fallen angels alike. These three factions have been locked in eternal conflict since the beginning of time."

"…This is all a bit hard for me to follow. I'm just a normal high school student. So is this what the Occult Research Club does?" Naturally, I just assumed Rias had been talking about the club's activities.

"The Occult Research Club is just a front. Think of it as my hobby. Its real purpose is to provide a place for demons to meet."

No, seriously… This has got to be just a club, right?

"Yuuma Amano…"

Hearing this name, my eyes snapped wide-open. How did Rias know about her?

"You went on a date with her, correct?"

"…If this is a joke, cut it out. I don't want to talk about that here." Unconsciously, a hint of anger had worked its way into my voice. Yuuma was still a sensitive topic for me. I mean, no one believed I dated her. No one even remembered her.

Everything about Yuuma had been a fantasy, an illusion. People wouldn't listen to me when I tried to tell them about her. They all just denied Yuuma had ever even existed.

I wasn't sure where or how Rias had heard about all that, but I was going to get really angry if she claimed to have learned of Yuuma through occult sorcery or some kind of nonsense.

"Oh, she exists. Most definitely," Rias declared. "Although, she has certainly tried to erase all evidence connecting the two of you." Rias snapped her fingers, and Himejima pulled a photograph from her pocket, handing it to me.

I was left utterly speechless at what I saw.

"That's her, isn't it? Yuuma Amano."

It was true. The picture was unmistakably one of my missing girl-friend, the girl who had vanished without a trace. I'd taken a photo of Yuuma with my phone before she disappeared, but even that was gone. Here, though, she had been captured perfectly. A pair of jet-black wings was sprouting from her back, though.

"This girl—this fallen angel... She's the same kind as the one who attacked you last night."

...A fallen angel? Yuuma?

"She made contact with you for the sake of her mission," Rias continued. "Once she had carried it out, she wiped all records of herself."

"Her mission?"

"Yes, to kill you."

—!

What the hell?!

"Wh-why would she want to—?"

"Calm down, Issei. It's nothing you did... Let's just say you were unlucky..."

"Unlucky?!" Was Rias saying it was nothing but a stroke of bad luck that had led to Yuuma killing me that day?!

Wait... Killed? But I'm still here, aren't I?

"You went on a date with her, and at the end, she killed you in the park with a spear of light."

"But I'm still alive! Anyway, why kill *me*?" There was no conceivable reason for anyone to do that to me. I had nothing to do with fallen angels or any of that nonsense!

"She had to get close to you to learn if you possessed something dangerous to them. I'm sure the response wasn't particularly strong, which is why it took her some time to confirm it. But then she found it. Your body is a vessel for a Sacred Gear."

A Sacred Gear... Those words sparked my memory.

"Sorry. Your existence poses a threat to us, you see. We had to take care of you quickly. If you want to blame someone, blame God for giving you that Sacred Gear in the first place."

That's what Yuuma had said. Did that mean one of those things was inside me?

"Sacred Gears are exceptional powers entrusted to certain humans," Kiba explained. "A lot of famous historical figures are believed to have possessed them. It's the power of their Sacred Gear that inscribed their names into the history books."

"Even today, Sacred Gears continue to appear in the world," Hime-jima continued. "I'm sure you've heard of great individuals playing important roles in society? Many of them possess Sacred Gears, too."

Rias took hold of the conversation again. "Most of these items aren't capable of much more than making a few waves in human society, but some have power formidable enough to threaten demons and fallen angels. Issei, raise your hand."

Huh? Raise my hand? Why?

"Quickly now," she urged me.

I lifted my left arm into the air.

"Close your eyes and visualize the most powerful thing that comes to mind."

"Th-the most powerful...? L-like Satoru's energy-wave attack from *Dragon Orb*...?"

"Very well, imagine that. Now picture it at its strongest."

"…"

Satoru's Dragon Wave technique appeared in my mind.

Am I doing this right?

"Slowly lower your arm and rise to your feet."

I did as she said and stood up from the sofa.

"Now put yourself in that stance. The absolute strongest pose, all right? Don't hold back."

Come on, Rias wants me to play make-believe Dragon Orb at my age? In front of everyone?! It was humiliating! Even with my eyes closed, I could see them all laughing at me!

"Come on," Rias pressed.

Arrrrrgh! Seriously? She really wants me to do it? Dammit! Fine, watch, but this is the only time! I put my hands together, one on top of the other, palms facing outward, arms outstretched.

"Dragon Wave!" I shouted.

"Now open your eyes. This room is overflowing with energy, so you shouldn't have much trouble manifesting the Sacred Gear."

Again, I did as Rias told me. My left arm was glowing. *Whaaaaat?! How is this possible? Did I actually pull it off?*

The light was beginning to take concrete form, enveloping my forearm. When it finally subsided, my arm was encased in some kind of red gauntlet. The ornamentation of the thing was very elaborate, like a piece of some high-quality cosplay outfit. A round, jewellike object was embedded in the part covering the back of my hand.

"Wh-what the hell?!" I screamed. I was utterly taken aback! Who wouldn't have been? I was trying to do a Dragon Wave, but instead, I triggered some sort of transformation sequence!

"That is your Sacred Gear. Now that you have manifested it, you can use it whenever you like."

This red gauntlet is a Sacred Gear?

Seriously…?

I still couldn't quite believe it. All I'd done was imitate an attack from a manga, and then…

"The fallen angel—Yuuma Amano—considered your Sacred Gear a threat, so she killed you."

It was all real. Everything with Yuuma, and all this Sacred Gear stuff, too.

Then I guess the same goes for the part where she killed me? How was I still alive, then?

"Moments before you died, you summoned me with this." Rias held up a leaflet.

I recognized the piece of paper. It was the one that weirdo had given me while I'd been waiting for Yuuma before our date.

The phrase *Your wishes granted!* had been scrawled over it like a catchphrase. A magical circle was also drawn on the handout. On closer inspection, it was identical in design to the huge one in the center of the room.

"That's one of our flyers. The magic circle serves to summon demons like us. Few people go through the trouble of actually drawing summoning arrays like that anymore, so we distribute these flyers for them to use instead. They're simple and convenient. One of my familiars was handing them out downtown that day, and you happened to pick one up. Then, on the brink of death after having been attacked by the fallen angel, you called out to me. It must have been a truly powerful wish to summon *me*. Usually, one of my servants like Akeno or the others here would have responded instead."

Well, I *had* just been impaled, so I guess you could say I was desperate. My hands were drenched in blood; maybe that's why the crimson-haired beauty, Rias Gremory, had come to mind. If that was the case, the redheaded figure I saw at the end of the dream—or whatever that vision was—had indeed been Rias.

"When you summoned me, I knew at once that you were a vessel of a Sacred Gear and that you had been wounded by a fallen angel. But that was where we had a bit of a problem. You see, those light-based weapons they use are just as deadly to humans as they are to demons. You were on the cusp of death. I decided to save your life."

Save my life? So Rias rescued me?

"You now exist as a demon. Issei, you have been reborn as an honored member of Rias Gremory's Familia, which means you are now my servant."

Whoosh!

All at once, wings burst forth from the backs of everyone around me. Unlike the black wings of the fallen angels, these were more leathery, like those of bats.

Whoosh. A strange sensation ran down my spine. When I glanced over my shoulder, I was startled to find the same kind of dark wings sprouting out of my own back.

Seriously? Me, a demon? Does that mean I'm no longer human?

"Let's start over. Yuuto?" Rias volunteered the only other guy to go first.

With that, Kiba turned to me with a wide grin. "I'm Yuuto Kiba. As you know, I'm a second-year student here like you. Um, and I'm a demon. Nice to meet you."

"…First-year…Koneko Toujou. Hello… I'm a demon, too," Toujou said softly with a bow of her head.

"Akeno Himejima, third-year. I'm the vice president of the Occult Research Club. It's a pleasure. I'm also a demon." Himejima let out a gentle giggle as she bowed in greeting as well.

Last was Rias. With a flick of her long, crimson hair, she proclaimed, "And I'm their master, Rias Gremory, of the ducal House of Gremory. We'll be working together from here on out, Issei."

What exactly have I gotten myself into?

Life.2
I'm Starting Out as a Demon!

"Hyaaaaaaaaah!"

I was pedaling my bicycle at full throttle through the dead of night. Why? To hand out leaflets complete with easy-to-use magic circles. When someone with a deep-set desire made a wish while holding one of those flyers, a demon like me would be summoned to answer their call.

I glanced at my cell phone. The screen showed a map of my surroundings, along with a blinking red dot ahead of me. That was where I was headed. Once I arrived at the place marked by that blip, I was supposed to chuck a leaflet in the mailbox before moving on to the next one—rinse and repeat.

"Damn, this sucks! But what choice do I have?!" I screamed, pedaling like a madman.

Let's go back for a minute, back to the day I first realized I had become a demon.

All within the span of a few minutes, I learned I was a bearer of a Sacred Gear, Yuuma was a fallen angel, and Rias was a demon.

As it happened, my own demon wings had vanished shortly after all those revelations. They would've just gotten in the way of my everyday life, after all. I'd been told I would be able to fly once I got used to them. Although, at the time, trying to move them did little more than make me feel sick… Look, having wings pop out of your back is a pretty huge shock.

"Serve me, and you will be in for a treat," Rias had promised with a wink before I'd even had a chance to get over the bewilderment of it all.

The way Rias spoke had made it sound like I had to live as her servant. Compensation for her saving my life, I guess. Humans who were reborn as demons had to serve the demon who granted them that reincarnation in the first place. Apparently, that rule was pretty absolute.

So I was a stooge… There were definitely worse fates than serving under a beautiful woman, but that still didn't make it easy to accept.

"Just so you know, demon society is divided into different strata. I have a noble title. In our world, one's status largely depends on birth and upbringing, but there are some demons who manage to climb the ladder. Everyone starts as a novice at first."

"Could you please stop talking as if this were a college recruitment?!" I complained. "Anyway, are you serious? This all sounds just a bit too weird."

Rias leaned over, putting her lips right against my ear. Her hair smelled wonderful. My brain went numb. Was this another of her demonic powers?

"Depending on how you play your cards, you could become *very* popular with the opposite sex."

—!

Those words sent my mind racing.

"How?!" The question burst out of my mouth before I even had a chance to think.

This could be a huge shot in the arm for my perverted desires! Wait, how do I know Rias isn't casting some sort of spell over me? I was way more excited than I should've been.

"Most pure-blooded demons perished in the Great War long ago. As a result, there was a critical shortage of loyal servants. The power and majesty that we used to possess when we stood at the forefront of our great legions were lost, too. Without fresh blood, we were doomed to perish. Just like with humans, there are male and female demons, and we are capable of bearing children. However, it would take eons for our numbers to recover through natural birth alone. Such a thing would leave us defenseless against the fallen angels. That's why we have been finding suitable humans and turning them into demons—as our retainers."

"So I *am* a stooge, then…"

"Oh, don't look so down. Let me get to the point. This conversion method only helps increase the total number of lesser-ranked demons. It doesn't bolster the number of powerful ones, so we introduced a system to give reincarnated demons—that is, those who were once human—a chance to rise up. If a reincarnated demon proves worthy, they will be granted a noble rank and title, regardless of how they were born. This system has really boosted our population. You might be surprised to learn just how many demons there are running around. Like the members of my club, there are plenty who have chosen to blend into human society, too. I'm sure you've met more than a handful of us already without even realizing it."

"There are *other* demons here?!"

"Yes. Some humans are able to detect us, but most can't. Those filled with powerful desires, or who want to make a deal, are better at sensing our presences. They're the type who usually summon us, using those leaflets that we hand out. Then there are others like you, who can tell us apart but can't bring themselves to actually believe we exist. Not until we show them our demonic powers anyway."

What?! So it was my overwhelming desire that summoned Rias as I lay dying?! In any event, it sounds like demon society has gone through a lot of changes. I'm sure it'd been pretty difficult for them, but honestly,

I didn't really care much about politics. What mattered was that I had been given a golden opportunity!

"S-so I can earn a noble title?!"

"Indeed. Anything is possible. Of course, it will take considerable time and effort."

"Whoaaaaaa!" I cried out. "Seriously?! Me?! I can make my own harem?! I can do whatever I want with them?!"

"If they're your servants, why not?"

A bolt from above may as well have struck me. I was ecstatic. *Seriously? I can actually do it?!*

Out in the real world, as a human, it was practically impossible to have a harem. As just some regular dude, I'd probably never be able to attract that many women. I mean, just take a look at my situation. I didn't even have a girlfriend. Heck, my last girlfriend murdered me.

But now the tides have turned!

"Whoaaaaaa! Being a demon is awesome! Hell yeah! I'm on fire! It's time to throw out all those magazines and—" I paused midsentence to think that over. "No, not the magazines. They're my most prized possessions. There's no need to get rid of them, not until Mom finds out anyway… Right, that's a separate issue!"

"You're a funny one." Rias chuckled with amusement.

"My, my. He's just like you said, like a dopey little brother." Himejima couldn't contain her gentle laugh, either.

Do these two just casually throw around insults?

"Anyway, Issei, you serve me now, understood? Don't worry; with strength like yours, I'm sure you will have no trouble distinguishing yourself. Who knows, you might even earn a title of your own one day."

"Understood, Rias!"

"No, no, no. That's President, got it?"

"President? What about Big Sis?" I asked half-jokingly. I'd always wanted an older sister in my life. Surely, I'm the only guy who has ever dreamed of calling an older woman Big Sis.

Rias frowned, giving the idea some real thought for a moment, before shaking her head. "Hmm, that does sound rather wonderful, but since we operate here at school for the most part, I think we should stick to President. This is the Occult Research Club, after all, and that is what everyone else calls me."

"Understood! Prez, teach me how to be a demon!"

Hearing this, Rias broke out into a truly devilish grin. She looked genuinely happy. "Hee-hee, an excellent response. Very good, Issei. I'll make a man of you yet." With that, she gently stroked my chin with her fingers.

M-my very own big sis! Under her tutelage, I'll awaken as a demon! Better yet, I'll rise up in the world!

All things considered, it was a pretty good deal. There was no going back to my human life, right? I just had to keep pushing forward!

This was how I found myself accepting my new situation. I don't care how stupid this might sound: I was completely fine with it all, or so I kept telling myself. This was my chance to push my perverted desires to the max.

Sure, I might've been getting too psyched, but as a sex-obsessed teenager, I had found my calling in life! Rather than dwelling on this strange, new reality I'd found myself dragged into, I resolved to simply live in the moment!

"I'll be a harem king!"

Reflecting back on how easily I'd taken it all in stride, I can't help but wonder if Rias had put some kind of spell on me. Even if she had, I wouldn't have cared that much. I was going to get my very own harem!

And that was how I became the newest member of the Occult Research Club.

Several days after starting life anew as a demon, I was pedaling my bicycle through the night, toiling away as Rias's toady.

First, we gathered late at night in our room in the old school building. After all, our demonic abilities were more powerful after dark. Yep, that strange rush that came over me every evening was my demonic potential. I was a true demon now, so my strength and energy skyrocketed in the darkness. It was a wonderful feeling, but it also explained why I was so weak in the mornings. Demons didn't handle light well. The brighter it was, the weaker we became. Light was poison—or so Rias said.

Angels, fallen or otherwise, used light-based weapons. This made them our natural enemies. I was warned that if I ever bumped into one of them, I was to flee immediately.

Supposedly, I would get used to the daytime. Mornings were so unbearably demanding because I had only just recently been reborn. Rias told me I'd grow accustomed in time. I guess that's why she left me alone for a while after that first time in the clubroom: so I could figure things out naturally, at my own pace.

It had always been her plan to contact me and reveal the truth when the time was right. In an eerie twist of fate, that suit-wearing fallen angel had come after me the very day Rias had planned to reach out.

Anyway, I was doing my best as a demon in Rias Gremory's service. Given how little I knew about demon society, the first thing I had to do was study up. Plus, as an underling, it had fallen on me to distribute the leaflets at night.

I had been worried that my parents would be furious about me being out so late, but Rias brushed away my concerns with a grin.

"I already took care of that back when I met them."

It must have been true, because they didn't get angry when I came home in the middle of the night after finishing my tasks. All they ever said was "Welcome home."

Yep, the prez's magic sure was amazing.

Speaking of amazing discoveries, the biggest surprise of all was finding out just how much power Rias held throughout Kuou Academy.

The school fell squarely in her territory, and she pulled all the strings behind the scenes.

From what I gathered, all the big shots in charge at the academy were connected to demons in one way or another. In particular, each was morally indebted to the Gremory family in some way. Basically, the campus was Rias's personal property, which explained why our club was able to use the grounds at night.

Anyway, let's get back to how my job was going.

Every night, I was supposed to cycle around town, stuffing leaflets, which would summon members of Rias Gremory's Familia, in each and every mailbox indicated on the strange phone she'd given me.

As far as I could tell, it was some secret technology born of demonic science. The thing was shaped like a portable game console. It had a touch screen, buttons, and a stylus. Displayed on the device's screen was a map of the town—Rias's territory.

In the human world, a demon was only permitted to work within their defined territory. *Work* meant getting summoned, forging pacts, granting wishes, and exacting payment. Fees were paid in the form of money, goods, or from time to time, the summoner's life.

That said, there weren't many people willing to go *that* far to make their wishes come true. When it did come up, the pact was usually called off, as such a payment wasn't worth whatever incredible thing the demon was offering.

"Not all human lives are of equal value," Rias had told me.

Man, the truth could hurt.

The dots blinking on the device indicated the homes of people possessed by overwhelming desires. My task was to go to each and every one of them and leave a leaflet so they could call on our services. So long as there were still dots flashing on that display, my job wasn't finished.

Now that I had become a demon, people didn't take much notice of me. Not even the police. I was practically invisible to human eyes as I went about my chores.

Though I spent every night biking around stuffing flyers into mailboxes, there were always more of those little red blips. People really were creatures of avarice. Once they'd received one wish, it became like an addiction. They were bound to summon us again.

In general, a pact could only be forged at night, as we demons were only permitted to work after dusk. Daytime was reserved for angels and God, though I still didn't really understand that part.

Anyway, each leaflet could only be used once. After it was spent, I had to go and deliver another. Which meant my drudgery would last forever. It was thanks to my efforts, though, that Rias and the others had an endless demand for work. We were certainly expanding our operations. If we kept on forging new pacts and granting new wishes, the demon king would be sure to recognize our worth.

So basically, if I kept this up, I had a shot at receiving a noble title of my own! *The more work, the better! The bigger, the better!* Whatever came my way, I wanted to forge a pact!

"Auuugh! I want to be surrounded by cute girls alreadyyyyyy!" I screamed into the night. However, there was little else for me to do but bide my time.

…But I couldn't help wondering just how long it was going to take.

After saying good-bye to Matsuda and Motohama—my two partners in crime—at the end of the day, I made my way to the old school building.

Originally, the job of distributing the club's leaflets around town had been assigned to Rias's familiars. She would transform mice or bats into humanlike forms and send them to do her bidding, day and night. The reason Rias assigned me such a menial task instead was because she wanted me to learn the ropes of demonhood from the bottom up.

Supposedly, Kiba and the others had been forced to do the same work, too, initially. He, Koneko Toujou, and Himejima all served Rias. Which made them my seniors. They all knew what it was like to be at the bottom of the heap. It was like that saying: *Every man has his history.* Or in this case, every demon.

It might not have been a huge deal, but I managed to convince Koneko Toujou and Akeno Himejima to let me call them by their first names. It was an important first step in getting them to accept me as an equal.

Heh-heh, I even made a point of calling out to them by name in front of Matsuda and Motohama. I'll never forget those guys' looks of resentment and chagrin. Of course, I hadn't told my two friends about what had happened to me. They wouldn't have believed me even if I did, and it would've been dangerous for them to step into my new world unprepared. Besides, I'd already died once. There was no reason to drag them into it and risk the same happening to them.

I chose to keep calling Kiba by his surname, by the way. That pretty boy could go to hell. There was no way I'd be getting all chummy with him!

Anyway, today I had been expressly summoned to the clubroom. I entered the now-familiar old school building and headed for the second floor.

"I'm here," I called as I stepped into the clubroom.

Everyone else had already arrived. The room was dark. The windows had been covered by heavy curtains, which completely shut out any natural light. The only bit of illumination came from the candles spread out over the floor.

"Good, you're here," Rias said, motioning to Akeno.

"Understood, President. Issei, will you step into the magic circle?" Akeno asked, gesturing to it with her hand.

An incredible beauty was waving to me! That was a wonderful reward in and of itself! I hurried into the center of the magic circle, eager for what would come next.

"Issei, you've handed out enough leaflets. Good work." Rias flashed a satisfied grin.

Does this mean my grunt work is over? I wondered.

"Now it's time for you to start your work as a demon in earnest."

"Awesome! So I get to make a pact?!"

"Indeed. Of course, as this is your first time, we shall start with a relatively simple one. Koneko has received two requests, you see. She can't do both, so we shall leave one to you."

"…Thanks for helping me out," Koneko said with a curt nod of her head.

So I'm gonna be taking on one of Koneko's jobs? It sounded simple enough. I was just about sick and tired of distributing leaflets. Pedaling my bicycle through the dead of night and throwing flyer after flyer into a never-ending stream of mailboxes was enough to leave me feeling pretty forlorn.

The other club members arranged themselves around the magic circle. Meanwhile, Akeno, who was standing in the center, began reciting some kind of incantation. Responding to her words, the magic circle began emitting a bluish-white glow.

"U-um…"

"Quiet now, Issei," hushed Rias. "Akeno is busy attuning the circle to your seal."

Ah right, my seal. Apparently, the huge magic circle in the center of the room was unique to the House of Gremory. For members of Rias's Familia, it was a bit like a family crest or coat of arms. When someone wanted to summon us or forge a pact, this symbol allowed them to reach us and no one else. Evidently, the activation of our demonic powers was inextricably linked to that symbol as well.

Kiba and the others each had their bodies marked in different spots with that same symbol, and it was essential for them to use their powers. I had thought about getting it on my body, too. Unfortunately, when first becoming a demon, you had to work out how to control your own powers before trying to using them in tandem with a supernatural phenomenon like a magic circle—or so I thought at the time anyway.

"Issei, hold out your hand."

I did as Rias instructed, offering her my left hand with my palm outstretched. She began tracing on it with the tip of her finger, and I wondered if she was casting some kind of spell. It didn't feel like she was doing anything more than just writing on my hand, when suddenly—

A brilliant light erupted from my palm. When it subsided, a light-blue symbol remained.

Whoa, my very own magic circle?!

"This is a teleportation circle. It will allow you to transport yourself to your client instantaneously, and when you're finished, it will return you this room."

Wow. That sounds pretty useful.

"Akeno, are we ready?"

"Yes, President." Akeno stepped outside the circle.

"Now stand in the middle," ordered Rias.

I did as she bade, and the symbol on the floor began emitting an intense, blue-green glow. I could feel the power welling up around me. Now that I was in physical contact with this large magical seal, the energy inside me was positively overflowing. Was this what it meant to be part of Rias's Familia?

"The magic circle is responding to the client. You will be able to jump there whenever you want. You know what to do when you arrive, I presume?"

"Yes!"

"A good response. Be on your way, then."

I was bursting with excitement! My first job! I would pull this off without a hitch!

The glow of the magic circle grew stronger and stronger. *So this is what it's like to teleport*, I thought. Soon, the light had completely engulfed my body. The brightness was so blistering, it forced me to close my eyes. I knew that when I opened them, I would be at my destination!

This is gonna be great!

And then in the blink of an eye, I was teleported away...

......

......

Huh? What the...? Was that it? Had it really ended that quickly? Nervously, I opened my eyes.

......

What I saw left me speechless.

I was still in the clubroom.

Huh? Wasn't I supposed to teleport? What about the client? I glanced at Rias. The crimson-haired beauty was resting her hand over her forehead, confounded.

"Oh dear," Akeno muttered with obvious disappointment.

Kiba, that bastard, let out a deep sigh. As frustrating as it was, something had clearly gone wrong.

"Issei," Rias called.

"Yes?"

"I'm sorry about this, but it looks like you won't be able to use the circle to jump to your client."

Huh? What's that supposed to mean?

"Using a magic circle requires a certain level of mastery over your demonic powers...," Rias explained in response to my evident confusion. "Not a great level of mastery, mind you. Actually, any demon should be able to pull it off, even a child. Warping with the help of a magic circle is the very first step in the life of a demon, after all."

Wh-what does that say about me...?

"In other words, Issei, you're not even at the level of a demon child. Your powers are so undeveloped that the circle won't respond to you. Your level is too low."

Wha—?

Whaaaaaaaaaat?!

"What the hell?!" I was at a loss for words. I couldn't teleport to the client because my abilities weren't good enough? Wasn't I supposed to be a demon?!

"...Pathetic," Koneko whispered, unfazed.

That's a pretty cruel thing to say, Koneko...

"Oh dear. This is a problem. What shall we do, President?" Akeno asked with a worried expression.

Boy, was I off to a bad start on my road to demonic success...

After pausing for a moment to think, Rias answered plainly: "We can't keep the client waiting. Issei..."

"Yes?!"

"We've never had to do this before, but I want you to go there on foot."

"On foot?!" I leaped up in shock. That was the last thing I was expecting her to say.

"Yes, just like you did when you were distributing the leaflets. I'm afraid we have no choice. You don't have any powers, so you'll have to make up for that in other ways."

"On my bike? You want me to go to the client on my bike? Are demons even supposed to do that?!"

Pshew. Koneko pointed her finger at me in mute silence.

Koneko... You sure know how to kick a man when he's down...

"Move along now! Forging pacts is a demon's job! We can't keep a client waiting!" Rias's face was unusually stern.

Ugh, why did I have to screw up on the very first step?!

"Auuuuugh! I'll do my best!" I all but ran out of the room, tears streaming down my face.

—○●○—

Riding through the dead of night, I sat atop my bike, bawling my eyes out. I was a demon who couldn't even respond to a summoning properly. To make matters worse, this predicament was apparently completely unheard of. My tears just wouldn't stop.

Saying I don't have any powers... What the hell was that supposed to mean?! At this rate, I'll never receive a noble title!

According to my cell phone, the destination was an apartment building at least twenty minutes from school by bicycle. Hopefully, the client was still home. If we were a delivery service, I would've no doubt faced the customer's wrath for the long delay.

Demonic services were usually rendered almost instantaneously, but I had ended up making the summoner wait more than twenty minutes. I'd have definitely been chewed out by my manager if this had been a regular job. Actually, my current boss *had* looked a little concerned. I guess that meant I'd disappointed her. I really wasn't suited to the life of a demon.

Finally arriving at the apartment, I loudly knocked at the door. "Hello! I'm from the demon, Madam Gremory! Sorry for the delay, but is this the right house?"

Even if I made a ton of noise, it shouldn't have been a problem. Demons could only be sensed by the person who'd summoned them. No matter how much of a disturbance I made, the client's neighbors wouldn't pay me any attention. When a demon was on assignment, they practically turned invisible to all outside parties. At least, that's what Rias had said.

"Wh-who's there?!" came a panicked voice from behind the door.

"Er, your demon. I'm new to the job, but, uh, you called, so I'm here."

"H-how stupid do you think I am?! Demons don't knock on the door! Koneko is supposed to come out of the magic circle on the flyer! Besides, you're not her!"

He was right, of course, and all I could do was beg his forgiveness. Neither I nor any of the others in the club had expected it to happen this way.

"Er, I'm really sorry. My demon powers aren't strong enough, so I couldn't go through the magic circle…"

"You're just some random weirdo, aren't you?!"

That struck a nerve.

"I'm not some weirdo! You think I wanted to come here like this?! I'd have used the magic circle if I could!"

"Don't get angry at *me*, you psycho!"

"Psycho?! What the hell?! I'm a demon, you hear me?!"

"Get out of here!" The door swung open. The client was coming to deliver his complaint directly to my face. He was a tall, skinny man. Overall, he appeared unhealthy. It looked like he was about to lay into me, but the second he saw my face, his expression softened. "…Are you crying?"

"Huh? Me?" I raised my hand to my cheek. It was wet.

"I see. So you were crying from shock because you couldn't teleport through the magic circle…"

"I guess so."

The client had let me into his apartment and even brought me a cup of tea. The whole thing with the magic circle had dealt a bigger psychological blow than I'd first realized, and I'd been bawling my eyes out completely unaware. When the client—a man named Morisawa—saw that, he'd felt so sorry for me that he invited me inside.

His apartment was clean and tidy. For a single guy, he kept it surprisingly tidy. When I asked, he told me he worked as a civil servant during the day. Morisawa was dedicated to his job, but his responsibilities left him craving more intimate social interactions, so he had turned to using the flyer to summon demons.

"So little Koneko couldn't make it…"

It sounded like Koneko had been the first to respond to his summoning, and Morisawa had been hooked on her ever since.

"Sorry, but it seems like she's pretty popular. I guess you could say she runs the cuteness department."

When using the leaflet to perform a summoning, a client could call the name of the demon they wanted to see. Again, I only knew this secondhand. Though Morisawa had called for Koneko, the job had been delegated to me. There were times when a client's requested demon was unavailable, and when that happened, someone else was asked to fill in.

"I—I was hoping for a cute demon, though…"

"I can act the part of a cute newbie. Would that be okay?"

"Ha! You're funny, you know that? If I had a holy sword on me, I would stab you for saying that!" Morisawa let out an amused laugh, but his eyes were stone-cold serious.

"By the way, if you don't mind me asking, what did you wish for when you tried to summon Koneko?"

Maybe I can still be of use. That hope, however, was shattered the moment Morisawa retrieved *the thing* in the corner of his room.

"I wanted her to wear this for me." It was a girl's high school uniform. Immediately, I had a feeling like I'd seen it before. "It's Kiyu Tanmon's uniform."

"Kiyu… Ah! From *The Melancholy of Akino Atsumiya*!" Even I knew about that series. The anime had been the breakout hit from last year. I'd watched it for a bit with my two negative influences, mostly just to see the female characters.

"Well then, demon, are you one of Tanmon's fans, too?"

"I'm more in Kako Yorumina's camp."

"Why is that?"

"Her breasts," I answered without any hesitation.

"—!" Morisawa was rendered momentarily speechless.

Kako Yorumina was another recurring character from the *Akino Atsumiya* series, a rich, voluptuous beauty.

"You like huge breasts, then?"

"Yep, my dreams are filled with them. My love cannot be overstated." In the back of my mind, I could imagine Rias's breasts bouncing up and down as she moved.

Prez, I fell in love with your cleavage at first sight. I'd be too embarrassed to say this to your face, but I'll protect those breasts of yours no matter the cost.

Morisawa broke into a lecherous smirk. "You have a good eye. I see you have a zeal for breasts as well. That means you've got the opposite of my own fetish. I prefer flat-chested characters, you see."

"I can appreciate that. One of my friends is the same." I was referring to my bespectacled buddy, Motohama. He was a true pervert, no doubt about it.

"Don't you think Koneko looks a lot like Tanmon? Her whole aura, I mean. I'll admit, she's a little on the short side, though."

Now that he mentioned it, Koneko was rather petite, expressionless, short-haired, and not particularly curvaceous. These were all qualities she shared with Kiyu Tanmon.

"That's why I wanted her to wear it! I really wanted to see it!" Morisawa wailed in frustration.

He sure seems disappointed. If he's that down about it...

"I understand. Maybe I could try wearing—"

"Don't you dare! I'll kill you!" Morisawa screamed indignantly.

He didn't need to get so emotional about it. I was just kidding, honest. Morisawa wiped away his tears as he calmed his breathing. After inhaling deeply, he said, "So what can you do? All demons have certain special skills, don't they? In case you hadn't heard yet, Koneko's is superhuman strength. She's an ace at literally sweeping me off my feet."

Hold on, she swept him off her feet? Well, I guess there are some guys in the world who are into that sort of thing. Anyway, as for my own special skill... Hmm... I crossed my arms as I gave it some thought. Solemnly, I answered, "I can do a Dragon Wave."

"Drop dead."

"Wha—?! What was that for?! And what's with that murderous look?!"

"What do you think it's for? What kind of demon has a special skill like that?"

"This one right here!" I shouted, pointing at my own chest.

"Do it then!"

"I will!"

"*Pssh*, if you even can! Just who do you think you're talking to? Back when I was a kid, we used to do Dragon Waves during lunch break every Monday. We even tried gathering energy so we could pull off Spirit Blasts. You'd better not be making light of my generation!"

"Shut up! Who cares if you saw it all firsthand?! I've got every volume of the manga! I've even got the first print of all the special editions! I practiced the Vanishing Technique in the schoolyard!"

If this guy wanted an argument, I was ready to give him one! Honestly, he was really getting on my nerves. Since he refused to believe me, I figured I'd just show him Issei Hyoudou's very own Dragon Wave!

I'll start by activating my Sacred Gear. I squeezed my eyes shut, lifted my left arm into the air, and pictured Satoru in the back of my mind… Then, as I lowered my arm, I adopted the Dragon Wave pose.

I'm putting my very soul into this, dammit! Eat this, old-timer fans! My ultimate attack!

"Draaagooon Waaaaave!"

My left hand sent out a sudden burst of light as the Sacred Gear appeared in the form of a red gauntlet that quickly expanded to cover my arm.

How's that?! That was a Sacred Gear for you! I glanced back to Morisawa, only to find he had burst into tears.

He got up and went to retrieve the first volume of *Dragon Orb* from his bookshelf. When he returned, he grabbed my hand tight and said, "We've got so much to talk about!"

Wha—?! This time, it was my turn to shed tears of joy. I knew exactly what Morisawa was saying; any true *Dragon Orb* fan would've.

"Let's get started!"

So began a long night.

*   *   *

"Ha-ha! Yep, I'm with you there. Oimoto really was the perfect voice for Kell!"

"Right? Like this line right here: *This is it!* It's perfect!"

We had been chatting cheerfully together over the manga for the past two hours. After Morisawa and I had gotten started, we completely forgot about the age gap between us. In a matter of minutes, we were practically best friends. Sure, Morisawa didn't leave a great first impression, but after we'd hit it off, the two of us were getting along famously.

"Well then, maybe it's time we got around to the pact?" Morisawa began.

"All right! You're the boss! Now what can I do for you?"

Yes! Things are finally turning my way! I had snagged my first pact! My quest for a noble title started here! The legend of Issei Hyoudou was about to begin!

"You probably get this all the time, but can you make me super-rich?"

Unsurprisingly, it was a pretty common wish.

"Understood. Let me see what I can do." I switched on my demon cell phone and flicked through the options. After putting the details into the calculator, the answer flashed up on the display.

"Ah, er, in your case, the cost for that wish would be your life. You'd have to die."

"Die?!"

"Yeah. Apparently, there's a saying among demons: *Not all human lives are of equal value.* Sorry. In your case, if you want to become rich, the tradeoff is your life."

"Th-that's gut-wrenching, you know? Fine then. Let's say I did wish for that. How would I die?"

"Um… Looks like you would drop dead just as a huge pile of money falls from the sky. You wouldn't even be able to touch it. Sounds pretty cruel, actually…"

"Guh! So I can't even slap you in the face with a wad of cash?!"

"Please don't hit me."

Yep, I had just crushed this man's dreams. For someone like Morisawa, a wish like that was asking the impossible. This must have been what Rias had meant when she said the world wasn't fair.

"All right then, what about a harem? What would happen if I asked for a feast of female flesh?"

Ooh, now we're talking! I was impressed. We were both men, after all, so it was a natural wish to have.

"Amazing! I love harems, Mr. Morisawa! They're every man's dream! I could drink to that wish! Although, I'm still too young…"

"Yeah, yeah, what does it say?"

I put the wish into my cell phone, but the outcome was just as rough as the first. "Er, it looks like you would die the second you laid eyes on them."

"I would bite it as soon as I saw them?!"

"Well, technically, you would die before you could even properly see how beautiful they were, I think. This is pretty awful, actually. You would probably be better off just watching beautiful women walking down the street."

"Arrrrrrrrrrgh!" Morisawa erupted into tears. "Am I really that worthless?! Ugh, I'm sorry I was even born…"

I patted him on the shoulder. "Let's keep talking about *Dragon Orb*. We can stay up until morning. Why don't we do a mock battle? I can be Satoru, and you can be Frieta. How does that sound?"

Morisawa, tears streaking down his cheeks, nodded his head. In the end, my first pact was a bust, and I spent the night comforting my dejected client.

—○●○—

"…"

Rias was clearly angry with me when I showed up at the clubroom after school the next day. She was staring my way with one eyebrow raised, in cold, mute silence. My face went pale. All I could do was stand there. I'd spent the previous night playing make-believe *Dragon Orb* with my client.

"This is unheard of," Kiba said with a forced smile.

"...Issei," Rias began in a low, foreboding tone.

"Y-yes?"

"You discussed manga with the client, and then what happened? Did you sign a pact?"

She was cutting straight to the chase. I could feel the sweat beading on my forehead.

"We—we called off the pact... A-and then we did a mock battle from a manga until morning!"

"A mock battle?"

"Y-yeah! Y-you pretend to be one of the characters and then start imagining how the fight would unfold!" What was I doing, explaining this so seriously? The thought of it made me want to cry. "I-I'm embarrassed about it myself. I mean, at my age... And as a demon, I *should* be embarrassed! I-I'll reflect on where I went wrong! I'm truly sorry!" I bowed my head low in apology.

Seriously, had there been any need to stay until morning?

"...After each pact, we ask the client to complete a questionnaire for us. You know: *How did you find our services?* The client can write their thoughts on the back of the leaflet, and they will appear here for us to read..." Rias paused there, holding out a piece of paper with Morisawa's feedback.

So we even have our own customer satisfaction survey? A demon's work is more involved than I thought.

"...*It was fun—more fun than I've ever had. I want to see Issei again. I should be able to come up with a better pact next time.* That's what it says."

"..." I felt a pleasant sensation welling up inside me.

Morisawa... I wasn't able to help him, and yet...

"I've never seen a response like this before. I didn't know what to do with it at first. That's why I must have looked a little foreboding when you came in."

So she isn't mad at me? Didn't I screw up the pact, though?

"For us demons, what matters most is that we enter into clear and precise pacts with those who summon us. Then we exact payment. That is how we have lived for a very, very long time…and now I don't know how to respond. I have never had to deal with a situation like this before. You have failed as a demon, yet the client was incredibly happy with you…" Rias wore a troubled frown for a moment but soon let out a faint smile. "One thing is for certain: You are an interesting one, Issei. I have never met a demon like you before. In terms of unpredictability, you might very well be my number one. Do try to remember the basic principles, though. You finalize pacts with clients, grant their wishes, and receive payment. Are we understood?"

"Yes! I'll do my best!"

She had forgiven me! That alone was enough to make me jump for joy.

Prez, I won't fail you next time!

—○●○—

Having reaffirmed my resolve, I set off to work again that night, pedaling full throttle toward my next client. This time, my destination was a residential complex roughly thirty minutes from school. I went as fast as I could, but the client was still forced to wait a whole half hour. I hoped the delay wouldn't put them in a foul mood.

Arriving at last, I ran up to the door and rang the doorbell. Having to stoop to the level of a common deliveryman was pretty mortifying for a demon.

I'll have to work out how to start using the magic circle soon…

"It's open. Show yourself in, meow," came an unusually throaty voice through the intercom. I wasn't even 100 percent certain whether it belonged to a man or a woman.

A man, maybe? And did he just say meow? I must have misheard him. I opened the door, slipped off my shoes at the entrance, and tiptoed furtively inside. The moment I stepped into the living room, my jaw may as well have hit the floor.

"Welcome, meow!"

I was faced with a humongous figure and an overbearing presence. Before me stood an enormous muscleman dressed in a Gothic Lolita outfit. On closer inspection, some of the buttons on the getup looked like they were ready to pop off, while in other places, the fabric appeared strained to the point of tearing in an effort to contain the wearer.

More than that, though, the guy's gaze was terrifying—yet somehow radiated pure innocence. Even more surprising was what he was wearing on his head.

Cat ears.

I gulped in trepidation. I could feel a bead of sweat sliding down my forehead. My hands were trembling in anxiety. This was no average guy—he was the embodiment of machismo!

Under the weight of such an intense aura, I couldn't help but feel as if I had waded into some kind of murder room. Every instinct told me to get out of there before I suffered a horrible death.

"Uh, er... I-I'm your demon... You summoned a demon from the House of Gremory...?" I asked fearfully.

There was a brilliant flash in the man's eyes as they lit up. The air itself seemed to be writhing in dread anticipation.

This is it! He's gonna kill me! Demon or not, I still raised my arms to shield myself.

"That's right, meow. I have a wish for you, meow," came the unexpected answer to my question.

Wait, so he really ends his sentences with meow? *Is that even legal?*

"Mil wants you to turn her into a magical girl, meow."

"You'll have to travel to a fantasy universe, then," I shot back immediately. Seriously, what he was asking was impossible. How was I supposed to grant a wish like that? I racked my brain, but it was beyond the realm of possibility.

And seriously? 'Mil'? That's what you're calling yourself?! This meathead's behavior was completely baffling. With a body like that, he could probably actually visit a fantasy universe and survive to tell the tale! In all likelihood, he could defeat a dark lord by himself!

"Mil already tried that, meow."

"You did?!"

"But it didn't work, meow. No one would give her any magical powers, meow."

"This whole situation is already pretty *magical*, though..."

"So now Mil is turning to her archnemeses, the demons, for help, meow."

So he already thinks of me as his enemy...? I'd better not respond to that, I thought.

"Mr. Demon!" The macho guy's voice—Mil's voice—was so powerful, it shook the whole room.

What is this? Some kind of word of power?!

"Mil wants fantasy powers!"

"This is already pretty fantastical! Look, you're gonna make me cry!"

That's when "Mil" actually burst into tears. *Dammit! Why do all my clients have to be complete weirdos?! What did I do to deserve this?!*

"Mil! Mil, calm down! Talk to me!" I still had a job to do, though. Something told me I had to find a way to calm Mr. Macho down and get whatever was bothering him off his chest.

Mil's intimidating face broke into a wide smile as he wiped away his tears. "Then let's watch *Magical Girl Milky Spiral 7 Alternative*, meow. That's where it all started, meow."

And so began another long night.

I was on my way home the next day after finishing my club activities at school when I let out a deep sigh. The prez had spoken to me with that strange half smile again. I had failed to secure a pact two nights in a row now. Yet, somehow, the feedback in both questionnaires had been first-rate.

I could tell the prez had been left bewildered by this unprecedented turn of events. Honestly, I was truly mortified that things just kept getting out of hand. As much as it pained me to admit it, my climb to success and a noble title of my own was far steeper than I'd first thought.

Last night, I had stayed up watching DVDs with Mil until morning. I hadn't taken it particularly seriously at first, but it wasn't long before the passion of the magical girls' performance and the moving plot opened my eyes to the wonders of the genre. Before I knew it, Mil and I ended up gleefully watching the series until sunrise.

Why do all my clients have to be such weirdos?

"Ah-ha-ha! Maybe Hyoudou's demonic power is to be chosen by clients like that?" Kiba had suggested while laughing with a sickeningly eloquent smile.

Go to hell, you worthless pretty boy! From what I'd heard, Kiba was frequently summoned by attractive older women.

Dammit! What kind of pacts does he make with them?! Are they after sex?! Just thinking about it made me want to strangle him. Curse you, Kiba!

"Aieeeee!"

Huh? I heard a sudden scream, followed by a dull plopping sound as something behind me tumbled to the ground. I looked over my shoulder and found a nun lying sprawled facedown on the ground, her arms outstretched. It was an almost unbelievably clumsy way to fall.

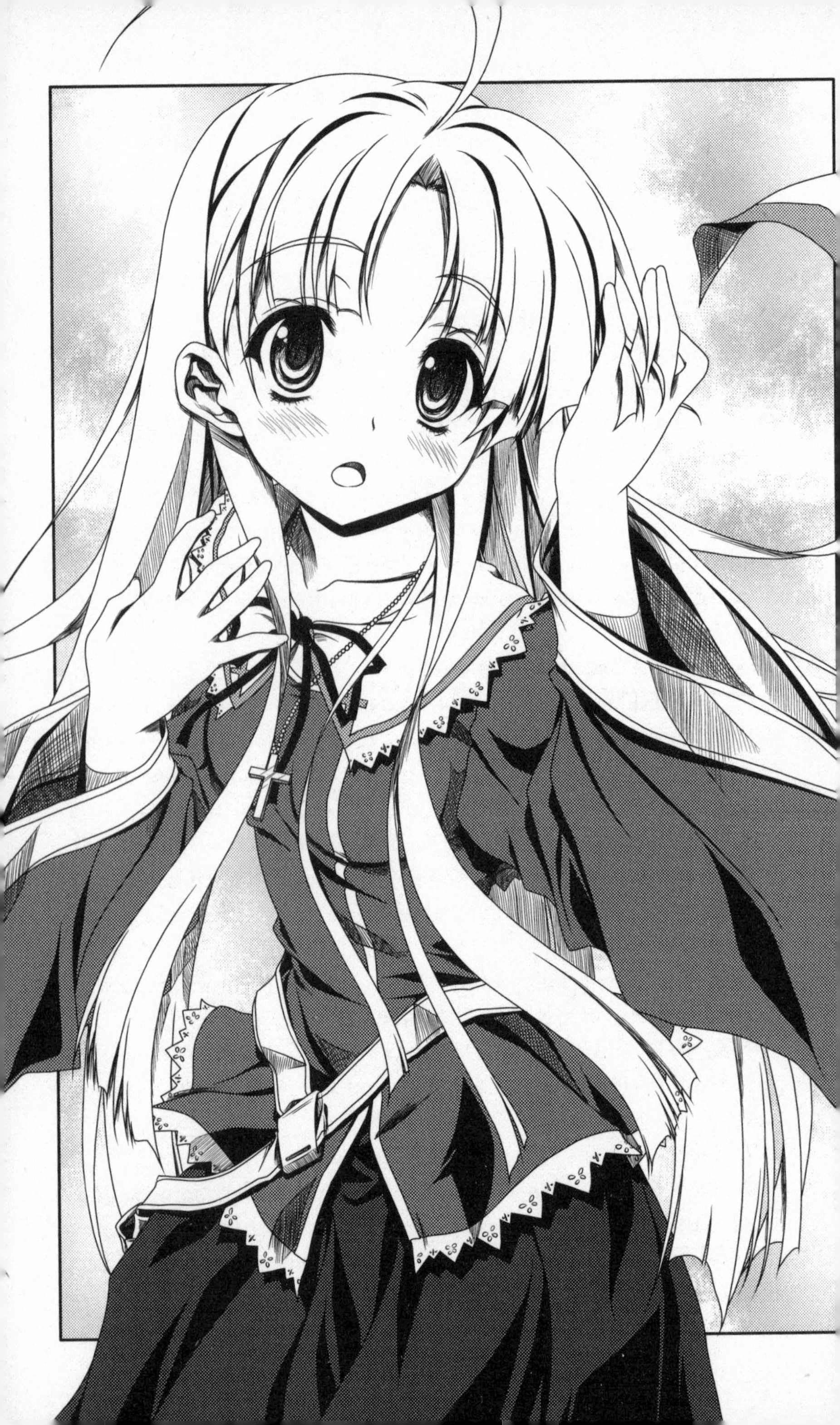

"...A-are you okay?" I asked as I approached her, holding out my hand to help her up.

"Owww. Why do I keep tripping...? Oh, I'm so sorry. Thank you!"

Judging by her youthful voice, she sounded like she was around my own age. I took her hand and helped her to her feet.

Whoosh.

A sudden gust of wind sent the nun's veil spiraling through the air. Her previously hidden blond hair fell down to her shoulders. The setting sun cast her locks in a brilliant radiance. Only then did my gaze shift to her face.

—!

In an instant, that blond beauty had stolen my heart. Her wonderful, green eyes were so enchanting, they seemed to suck me right in.

......

For a short while, all I could do was stare at her.

"U-uh... Is something wrong...?" she asked worriedly as she looked back at me.

"Oh. S-sorry. Er..." I couldn't bear to continue. There was no way I could tell her what I was really thinking. *You're ravishing! I'm in love!* Yeah, no way. I mean, she was *it*—the spitting image of my ideal beauty—the blond version anyway! I was utterly enchanted!

I've gotta make sure the conversation continues. Was this a heads-up from fate that this magnificent blond would play some important role in my life, or was I just deluding myself?

Then I noticed the travel bag hanging from her shoulder. Actually, now that I thought about it, a nun was a pretty rare sight in my town. I don't think I'd ever met one before.

Anyway, first things first, I went to pick up her veil. Fortunately, it hadn't landed too far away.

"A-are you a traveler?" I asked nervously.

"No," the nun answered with a shake of her head. "I've actually just been assigned to the church in this town... Do you live here? I'm so happy to meet you." With that, she bowed her head in greeting.

Oh, so she got transferred? I guess even houses of worship have personnel changes. It must be a hard life, I thought.

"I've had a bit of a problem ever since I arrived… I can't speak Japanese very well… I get lost all the time and can't really understand what everyone is saying…" She clutched her hands together at her chest, her face flushed with embarrassment.

…I guess that means she can't understand Japanese.

If that was true, it was probably because I was a demon that I'd been able to communicate so easily with her. The prez had said something about that not too long before I ran into the nun.

"Language is one of a demon's skills. The moment you became one of us, you gained the ability to converse with anyone in the world. Anyone hearing you speak will understand you in the language in which they are most comfortable. An American would hear you in English. A Spaniard in Spanish. The opposite applies as well. If they speak in a foreign language, it will sound like Japanese to you."

So this was what she meant.

In my English class at school, I had understood everything in perfect Japanese. I had been completely taken aback. When the teacher asked me to read a passage out loud, I left my classmates staring at with me mouths agape. It was understandable. Out of nowhere, I had become 100 percent fluent in English. Even the teacher didn't know how to respond.

That said, I couldn't read any of the English text. This ability was limited to spoken language, apparently. Still, that was more than enough. Just being able to converse with anyone anywhere in the world was incredible. Basically, I had become an unqualified international student.

"I think I might know where your church is," I said to the nun. I recalled there being an old church-like building on the outskirts of town. Maybe that was it?

But does anyone still visit that place?

"R-really?! Th-thank you! Praise the Lord!" The young nun gave me a brilliant smile as tears flowed from her eyes. She really was cute.

Suddenly, some incredibly negative feeling washed over me when I saw the rosary hanging around her neck. I guess that made sense. I was a demon now, after all. Usually, a nun and someone like me weren't supposed to have much to do with each other. Still, I couldn't just leave an innocent young lady alone in distress.

Leading the way, I guided the blond nun to the old church.

We cut through a park on our way to the chapel when we heard a child's cry.

"Waaaaah!"

"Are you all right, Yoshi?"

The boy was with his mother, so he should have been fine. He'd only fallen over. Nonetheless, the nun, who until now had been following behind me, headed deeper into the park, toward the sound of the kid.

"Hey, what are you doing?" I took off after her.

The nun approached the crying boy sitting flat on the ground. "Are you okay? Boys shouldn't get so worked up over something like this, you know," she said as she patted him gently on the head. The kid probably couldn't understand what she was saying. Still, he could see the blond nun's face overflowing with kindness. She placed her hand softly against the scrape on his knee.

What happened next came as a total shock. A faint, green light erupted from the flat of her hand, enveloping the boy's injury.

Huh? Magic? The prez had said that only demons and the humans working with them could use powers like that, though. As I watched, the abrasion on the boy's leg began to fade away. Was the light from the nun's hand healing it? Something clicked in the back of my mind.

A Sacred Gear. "Exceptional powers entrusted to certain humans"—

that was how Kiba had described them. I could sense my hunch was right. Looking at that glow emanating from the nun's hand made my own arm throb in response.

Is my Sacred Gear resonating with hers? Is this some kind of reaction? When I looked closely, the boy's scrape was completely healed, leaving no visible sign of injury. It was incredible.

So this is the work of a Sacred Gear... Apparently, they could come in all shapes and sizes.

The boy's mother was stunned. No doubt anyone would've reacted that way seeing something so unbelievable happen before their very eyes.

"There we go, all better now," the nun said, patting the boy's head again. She glanced up at me. "Sorry for wandering off," she laughed, sticking out her tongue playfully.

The boy's mother, regaining her composure, quickly took him by the hand and hurried away. "Thank you!" the boy called out in gratitude.

"He said thanks," I translated, and the nun broke out into a warm smile. "By the way," I began, "that power you have..."

"Yes. I can heal people. It's a wonderful gift, given to me by God." She smiled back at me, but there was a hint of sadness in her eyes. I got the feeling the nun's ability had also been the cause of some difficulty for her.

Probably best not to pry, I thought. This wasn't the time or place to blurt out that I possessed a Sacred Gear, too. They were unique abilities, and I could imagine that some people had to endure considerable hardship because of them. I hadn't exactly been particularly pleased when the Sacred Gear first enveloped my arm, either. The whole experience was pretty distressing, actually. To make it worse, I still didn't even know how to use it, so there wasn't much to be happy about. Pretty much the only thing it had been good for was pulling off a Dragon Wave.

Our conversation turned to silence, and we continued toward the church. It only took a few minutes before we reached the site of the old building. It had definitely been a church at one point, but it was just as dilapidated as I remembered.

I'd never heard of anyone using the building before, but I could see lights coming from inside. Someone was clearly in there.

A sudden chill ran through my body. It was the same sensation I'd felt when seeing the rosary but stronger. The reason was easy enough to grasp. I was a demon, which meant a place dedicated to God and angels was enemy territory. The prez had given me a stern warning not to go near any shrines, temples, or churches.

"Ah, this is it! Thank goodness!" After glancing back at her map and notes, the nun heaved a sigh of relief. It really *was* the right place. That was good to hear. I got a strong impression it was a bad idea for me to hang around any longer than necessary. It was almost nightfall, so it was time to get going.

The thought of having to drag myself away from such a beautiful young woman was painful. But I was a demon, and she was a nun. A budding love that transcended the boundaries between us would indeed have been romantic, but we weren't at that level.

Seriously, though, that church was giving me the shakes. My whole body was trembling.

Demons must have an instinctive fear of places like this, I thought. I felt like a frog being watched by a snake—or rather, a frog that, having been encircled by a snake, stood frozen in terror.

"I'll be on my way, then," I declared.

"Wait, please!" The sister called out behind me as I turned to leave. "Please allow me to show you my gratitude for bringing me here. Won't you join me inside?"

"Sorry, I'm in a bit of a rush."

"Oh, that's…" Her face was troubled. She'd probably wanted to make me a cup of tea to say thanks. However, given my circumstances, that was just too risky. As much as it pained me to do so, I had to decline.

"My name's Issei Hyoudou. Everyone just calls me Issei. What's yours?"

The sister responded with a wide smile. "Asia Argento! Please call me Asia!"

"Well then, Sister Asia. I hope I see you again sometime."

"Yes! Issei, me, too!" she said, bowing her head deeply.

I waved good-bye. Asia watched until I turned a corner and disappeared from her line of sight. She was a good person. That much I could tell on intuition alone, and I was sure this fateful meeting was nothing short of destiny.

—o●o—

That night, in the clubroom, the prez's expression was even sterner than usual. "Don't go anywhere near that church again," she scolded me. She was truly angry this time.

"Churches are hostile places to us demons. Taking even one step inside could have fatal ramifications for relations between our side and theirs. It looks like the angels decided to look kindly on you this time since you were helping one of their servants, but remember that they are always on alert. It wouldn't have been surprising if a spear of light had been hurled your way."

...*Seriously? Had the situation been that dire...?* Thinking back on it, that sense of dread that had fallen over me had been pretty extreme. That must have been what the prez meant when she said we could sense danger. My demon instincts had been trying to warn me.

"Don't involve yourself with anyone even remotely connected to the Church. Exorcists, in particular, are our mortal enemies. They carry God's blessing and are capable of destroying us at will. Even more dangerous are exorcists in possession of Sacred Gears. You were brushing up against death there, Issei." Rias paused, her gaze boring into me as she brushed her hair back with a hand. The prez's eyes carried an intense weight. She wasn't fooling around.

"O-okay…"

"You escaped death as a human by being reincarnated as a demon, but an exorcist will extinguish your life completely. You will be reduced to nothingness. Absolute nothingness. No consciousness, no existence. Do you realize what that means?"

Nothingness… Frankly, I couldn't even comprehend it.

Seeing my distressed reaction, the prez shook her head. "Sorry. Perhaps that was a little harsh. In any event, watch your step."

"I will…" That marked the end of our conversation.

"Oh my. Have you finished lecturing him?"

"Wha—?!" I jumped when I realized that Akeno had been standing behind me. All she did was give me her usual cheerful grin. I hadn't even known she was there.

"What is it, Akeno?" Rias asked.

Akeno's expression clouded slightly. "The archduke has requested that we embark on a hunt."

—◯●◯—

A stray demon—such a thing did exist. It was exceptionally rare, but every now and then, someone who'd been reincarnated as a servant demon would betray or murder their master. Demons were endowed with great power—much greater than they could ever have possessed back when they were human. It stood to reason that there were some who wanted to use those abilities for themselves, leaving their master's side and running wild. Such demons were known as strays. Actually, that fallen angel in the suit, Dohnaseek, had mistaken me for a stray.

Runaway demons were trouble. When they were found, their former masters, and sometimes other demons, were called on to eliminate them. That was another law by which demons lived. On top of that, angels and fallen angels alike regarded strays as a threat, too, and would slay any such demon on sight. There was nothing more terrifying than a demon who had decided to shed their restraints.

The prez, Kiba, Akeno, Koneko, and I had all come to an abandoned building on the outskirts of town. Word was a stray demon had been luring people here each night to feed on them. As such, we had been instructed by a high-ranking demon to take care of the problem.

"She has fled to your territory, Rias Gremory, so I want you to eliminate her."

This was just another part of a demon's work. Still... To think there were demons vicious enough to feed on humans...

No, hold on. That does sound par for the course for a demon. Maybe they only behave themselves because of their laws...

It was late. The world was blanketed in darkness. Wading through a field of tall grass, we approached the site of the attacks. The abandoned building slowly took shape in the distance.

With my demon eyes, I had no trouble making out the structure.

Y'know...enhanced vision isn't as great when you have to look at such a spooky place...

"...I smell blood," Koneko murmured, covering her nose with the sleeve of her uniform.

Blood? I couldn't smell anything. I guess that meant she had a good nose.

Silence descended on us. There was an evil, murderous presence somewhere nearby. My legs were trembling. I was seriously terrified. If the others hadn't been with me, I would have turned tail and fled. Thank goodness for the prez! She was standing confidently, hands on her hips, as our vanguard!

"Issei, this will be a good chance for you to learn how to fight," Rias said nonchalantly.

"Wh-what? Are you serious? Wh-what do you expect me to do?!"

"Yes, I suppose you're right." The immediacy of her take-back just made me feel even worse.

"But you *will* be able to watch us. For today, at least, observe how we fight. Ah yes, I should also explain my servants' attributes and classes."

"Attributes? Classes?" I repeated dubiously.

"Demons can bestow special characteristics on their servants... Yes, I suppose this is as good a time as any to tell you a little about our history."

So the prez began explaining how it came to pass that demons had reached their current state.

"Long ago, we demons were involved in a three-sided war against the fallen angels and the armies of God. All three factions possessed incredible power and had been engulfed in a bitter struggle against one another for an eternity. As a result, each side exhausted its manpower and resources. The conflict drew to a close several hundred years ago without a clear victor."

Kiba picked up from where Rias left off: "The demons suffered considerable losses, too. Those with noble titles would have normally commanded twenty or thirty loyal troops, but most of those soldiers were lost in battle. Their numbers had declined so drastically that they couldn't even field a real army anymore."

Next, it was Akeno's turn: "It is said that a great many pure-blooded demons died during that time. But even now that the war is over, demons, angels, and fallen angels still detest one another. Even taking into account that the other sides lost the brunt of their forces, too, we still can't afford to let our guard down around them."

The prez wrapped it up: "And so the demons adopted a new system based on a small but elite corps: Evil Pieces."

"Evil Pieces?" This sounded complicated, so I did my best to pay attention.

"The demon nobility based it on the human game of chess,

mimicking the attributes of the various pieces and bestowing them on their servants. There was a bit of irony intended there, as most servants are reincarnated humans. Since that decision, chess has become quite popular among us as well, but let's put that aside for now. Master demons, like myself, are the King. Below that, there are five classes corresponding to the Queen, Knights, Rooks, Bishops, and Pawns. Since we no longer possess great armies, we grant these exceptional abilities to a handful servants. This system has been in place for hundreds of years now, but it has proven very popular among the nobility."

"Popular? We're talking about chess here, right?"

"They started competing against one another. *'My knight is strongest!'* one would say. *'No, my rook is better!'* another would counter. That sort of thing. High-ranking demons began using their servants to play a real-life version of chess among themselves. The call it the 'Rating Game.' In any event, it's quite popular. There are even tournaments. The strength of one's pieces and one's ability to strategize can influence one's rank and title. There are those who make a point of gathering exceptional humans to themselves to use as pieces, too. Extraordinary servants are a mark of status, you see."

So being skilled in the game is the hallmark of a great demon...and a source of pride, I reasoned.

...Hmm, so former humans have been turned into servants to be used as pieces in a game. I didn't know how I felt about that. Would I be forced to compete one day, too?

"I'm still inexperienced, so I haven't been able to compete in any official tournaments yet myself. Even if I was allowed, there are a lot of conditions that have to be cleared before one can enter. In other words, you and the others here won't be participating for some time."

"Does that mean Kiba and the others have never played before, either?"

"Yes." Kiba nodded.

Demon society sure was strange. That stereotypical image of wicked creatures was crumbling in my mind. Though, perhaps that was overly naive. Either way, there was something else bothering me. What piece was I, exactly?

"Prez, what about my piece? What's my class and specialty?"

"Indeed. Issei—" But Rias stopped there. I knew why. Dread chills were coursing down my spine.

The sense of danger and foreboding that had been hanging over us for some time had suddenly grown stronger. Something was approaching! Even I, who had only just been reborn as a demon, could tell that much.

"What *is* this stench? Gimme a taste! Sweet? Bitter?" This hushed voice was coming from somewhere close to the ground. Something about it made my skin crawl and filled my mind with fear.

"Stray demon Byser! We have come to extinguish your life," Rias fearlessly declared.

"Kee-hee-hee-hee-hee-hee-hee-hee…" An ominous, raspy laugh echoed around us.

Now I understood. That laughter wasn't human, nor did it belong to a demon anymore.

The figure of a woman, naked from the waist up, floated up from the shadows. No, this thing was more than that.

Thump.

Heavy footsteps echoed in the night. The next thing I knew, a gigantic beast appeared before me. It was an unnatural, grotesque creature composed of a woman's torso, head, and arms. Beneath these sat the body and legs of a monster. The creature was grasping something in both hands that looked an awful lot like a lance. Its lower body boasted four wide, powerful legs, complete with razor-sharp claws and a serpent's tail that was moving independently!

This horrible thing had to have stood at least five meters high—even taller if it reared up on its hind legs. No matter how you looked at it, the thing was the real deal, a monster.

Is this really a demon? It has to be, right? Rias called it a stray. To think such creatures actually existed! The reality of this whole demon thing was finally starting to dawn on me!

"Forsaking your master and rampaging to please your own base cravings is a crime deserving of death. In the name of Duke Gremory, I shall gladly bring an end to your miserable existence!"

"How impertinent! I'll tear you to pieces, girl, and dye your body the color of your crimson hair!"

The creature's howl filled the night air, but Rias merely snorted in amusement.

"All bark and no bite. Yuuto!"

"Okay!"

Kiba, who'd been standing next to me, rushed forward at Rias's order. He was fast—incredibly fast. My eyes couldn't even keep up with his movements!

"Issei, let's continue where we left off," Rias lectured.

Huh? Does she mean about the Evil Pieces or whatever?

"Yuuto is a Knight, so his attribute is speed. Knights specialize in agility, you see."

Just as the prez explained, Kiba moved faster and faster until he was too quick for the eye to see anymore. The monster lashed out again and again with its lance but couldn't seem to find its target.

"Yuuto's greatest weapon is his sword," Rias continued.

Kiba came to a sudden halt, and in his hands was a large, European-style sword, gleaming in the night's faint light as he drew it from its sheath. In a flash, he disappeared again. That very same moment, the monster let out a thunderous cry of pain.

"Gyaaaaargh!"

Both of the creature's arms, along with the lance still gripped in its hands, had been cleaved from its body. Blood gushed from the cuts.

"Those are Yuuto's abilities: incredible agility and masterful swordsmanship. By combining these two attributes, he makes an excellent Knight."

Wait, what's that shadow moving around the wailing monster's legs...? Koneko?!

"Next up is Koneko. As a Rook, her attributes are—"

"I'll crush you!" the monster howled as it brought one of its tremendous legs crashing down.

K-Koneko! It certainly didn't look good for the quiet girl... But that stray demon's powerful limb never reached the ground. Instead, petite, little Koneko was holding its leg up with her bare hands.

"A Rook's attributes are simple. Unbelievable strength and an impenetrable defense. A demon like that could never hope to harm Koneko, much less actually crush her."

With an effortless heave, Koneko tossed the monster into the air, leaped up after it, and delivered a powerful punch right into its abdomen.

"...See you." The abomination's enormous body was sent flying backward.

I suddenly recalled what my client, Morisawa, had said the other day: *"All demons have certain special skills, don't they? In case you hadn't heard yet, Koneko's is superhuman strength. She's an ace at literally sweeping me off my feet."*

This was superhuman all right! Koneko had somehow sent that immense monster soaring with a single punch! I made a note not to cross her. She could probably kill me with her pinky finger. Koneko had a truly terrifying skill set, and the fact that Morisawa was so infatuated with her was just as frightening.

"Lastly, we have Akeno."

"Yes, President. Oh dear, what shall I do?" Akeno let out a light chuckle as she approached the fallen creature.

"Akeno is a Queen. Next to me, she is the strongest piece. She is the indomitable vice president of our little club, complete with all the attributes of a Pawn, Knight, Bishop, and Rook combined."

"Grrrrr..." The monster glared toward the beautiful, black-haired girl.

Akeno, however, met the scowl with a dauntless smile. "Oh dear, you *are* a stubborn one. How about this, then?" She raised both hands into the air, and then…

Bang!

The next moment, there was a brilliant flash as a bolt of lightning struck the stray demon.

"*Gaaaaaaaaaargh!*" The beast let out an earsplitting shriek at the force of that electric shock. Its entire body was left badly burned, and smoke wafted into the air.

"Oh dear, are you still rearing to go? It looks like you can take another one."

Bang! Another burst of lightning smashed into the creature.

"*Gyaaaaaaaaaargh!*" The bolt earned another deafening wail. It sounded like the monster was in its death throes. Regardless, Akeno relentlessly hit it with a third blast.

"*Gwaaaaaaaaaargh!*"

Akeno's expression as she brought down strike after strike was filled with cold derision.

Wha—? Is she laughing? Akeno's actually enjoying this?

"Akeno excels at using her demon powers to attack. Lightning, ice, fire—she can turn any natural phenomenon into a weapon to wield against her foes. She is also the ultimate dom."

A dom?! She's a sadist?!

"Though usually quite kindhearted, once she allows herself to get caught up in the heat of battle, no one can stop her until she has had her fill."

"…Ugh, Akeno. That's actually pretty unnerving…"

"There's no need to be afraid of her, Issei. She can be sweet and caring when it comes to her friends. I even heard her call you cute once. You should let her pamper you. I'm sure she would be more than happy to embrace you."

"Hee-hee-hee. I wonder just how much you can take? Now, now, my

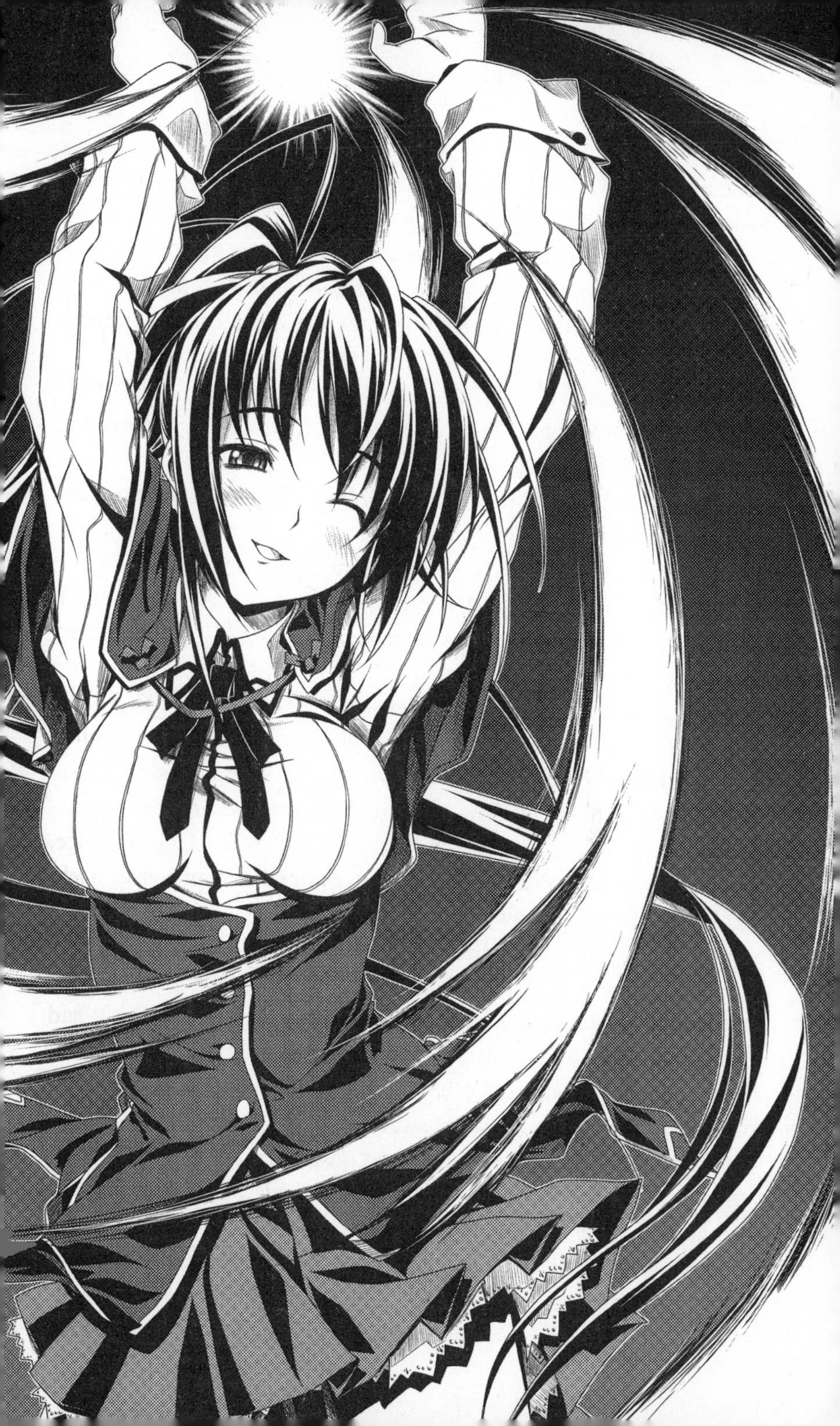

dear monster. You can't die yet, do you hear me? It's my master who will finish you off! Oh-ho-ho-ho-ho-ho-ho!"

...Prez, please don't leave me alone in the same room as this woman...

I'd thought Akeno was the most sensible of the group, but after seeing her in action, there was no doubt she was a demon. Terrifyingly so.

Akeno continued to loose one strike of lightning after another for the next few minutes. When Akeno finally brought her breathing under control, the prez gave her a brief nod.

Rias approached the fallen creature, now completely unable to offer any resistance. The prez lifted her hand toward the monster, which lay facedown, and asked: "Do you have any last words?"

"Kill me..." was all it could say in reply.

"So be it." Rias's response was ice-cold. A deathly chill coursed down my spine.

A gigantic mass of deepest darkness emerged from Rias's hand, large enough to engulf the monster completely. Immediately, it enveloped the creature. When the conflagration of demonic energy dissipated, the monster was gone. Just as Rias had promised, she had completely extinguished it.

After confirming the deed was done, the prez let out a deep sigh. "That's all. Thank you, everyone."

The others returned to their usual selves. I took that to mean the hunt was over.

So this is the fate that awaits strays. I didn't know what to say. What could that thing have been thinking, leaving its master knowing *this* would be the consequence? What's more, the battle had been absolutely ferocious. It was clear to me then that there was still a lot I had yet to learn about being a demon—and about my new companions, too.

If this is my competition, I'll have to aim high... It'll probably take me decades to climb the ranks. My mind went back to Rias's previous explanation of the Evil Pieces. Since I served a noble demon, it stood to reason that I'd been given one of those roles, too.

"Prez, there's still something you haven't told me…"

"And what would that be?" Rias answered with an amused smile.

"About my Evil Piece… Or I guess, my role in your Familia…"

Truth be told, I was already bracing myself for the worst. I knew what the answer would be. But still, I had to hold out hope. There were two options left. Akeno was the Queen, Koneko the Rook, and Kiba the Knight. Which left the Bishop…and the Pawn.

I'd held out for as long as possible but didn't have long to wait before my hopes were completely, utterly dashed.

With a broad grin, the crimson-haired Rias answered: "A Pawn. You're my Pawn, Issei."

I was the lowest possible rank.

Life.3
I Made a Friend!

"Ah… The road to success sure is a long one…," I muttered as I stared up at the ceiling of my bedroom.

A Pawn—that was what I was, my role, my class. A Pawn—the lowest possible position.

How was I supposed to rise up from all the way down here…? No sooner had I set out on this journey than I had been dealt a bloody nose.

Incidentally, it seemed Rias already had a Bishop. A short time after the battle, she'd said to me, "My Bishop role is already taken, but they aren't here right now. I've sent them elsewhere on a mission but will introduce you when we have a chance."

Who's "they," exactly? I hope it's a girl at least. Maybe I'll meet the Bishop soon?

In any case, I had been assigned the dregs, the Pawn. Yep, my prospects weren't good.

Am I really okay with this?

I had been murdered by a spiteful fallen angel all because of this Sacred Gear, one that was good for nothing but doing a Dragon Wave, and my first love had all been a sham. Plus, I'd been turned into a demon.

Sure, it had been a beautiful demon who'd scooped me up and made me her servant, but did she even ask if that was what I wanted? She'd even deceived me with the promise of my very own harem.

I had been slaving away for her since then. Every day, I'd been handing out leaflets and trying to forge pacts, yet my demon powers were still so paltry, I couldn't even teleport to meet my clients. As a demon, I was prodigiously pathetic.

I took a deep breath.

Now that I thought about it, I'd never had any special skills or abilities, even before becoming a demon. I'd tried everything I could think of to score with the opposite sex, but in the end, I just couldn't win against those damn popular pretty boys.

All my life, I'd never really had any dreams I'd been striving for, either. At least becoming a demon had given me something to work toward.

Hold on, has being turned into a demon actually been a good thing for me?

If Rias hadn't saved me, my life would've been over. Now I had another chance to savor my youth. I had to admit…it *was* fun. I was surrounded by beauties each and every day, and they were all so kind to me. Kind for demons anyway.

Rias was stunning, and Akeno wasn't too bad, either, so long as I didn't get on her bad side. Koneko also wasn't a problem, provided as I didn't do anything weird. Kiba might have been a bit of a pain, but he was willing to have normal conversations. Even if he was a pretty boy…he was a nice enough guy.

I guess you can't judge people by appearances, I thought. *I might have to rethink my attitude toward popular types.*

Then I remembered the adorable, blond nun I'd met the other day, Asia. She sure was lovely. If I could go out with her… But I stopped myself there and held my head in my hands. I had already experienced one unrequited love.

Dammit, Yuuma, playing with my heart like that... I was really into you. Why is someone else always pulling the strings in my life? I started wondering if maybe that's just how life worked. There had been so many strange things happening around me that I'd basically just been dragged from one unbelievable circumstance to the next.

Sister Asia... It was hard to think of someone in a more dissimilar position than me. *I'll probably never see her again anyway.* She had her own path to follow, and I had mine.

I was a thrall to a demon, and she was a servant of God. It had been nothing more than a chance encounter. Not bumping into each other again was probably for the best. It was only likely to make us both unhappy.

"Man, I'm a useless Pawn... Am I even capable of earning a noble title...? How about it, Mr. Demon King? I guess there's no point even asking." I let out a forced laugh. I needed a goal.

Wait, that's it! I'll find a way to use the teleportation circle! That would be my first step on the road to greatness! Yep, I was getting fired up now! The time for feeling sorry for myself was over. I was a demon, and nothing was going to change that.

As such, I resolved to live my demonic life to the fullest. I would make my dreams come true. Even if I couldn't, my life's goal would be to try.

All right! I can do this!

Soon after, night—the time when demons awakened—arrived.

I pedaled my way through the darkness, this time not to an apartment or residential complex but to an ordinary house. This was my first assignment like this, so I wasn't entirely sure what to do.

Since the client didn't live alone, wasn't there a chance I'd be seen by their family? I mean, I was coming in person. Even if strangers weren't supposed to be able to see me, did that apply to family members, too?

Regardless, I didn't have much choice, so I went to ring the doorbell, only to suddenly realize the door was already open.

…That's a pretty irresponsible thing to do at night.

Ba-dump.

I was struck by a sense of foreboding. An ill premonition swept over me. Nonetheless, I remained determined and took a step inside. I peered in through the entryway. There were no lights on in the hallway. A staircase led upward, but it, too, was pitch-black. The only light came from a single room on the first floor toward the back of the house, the door of which was slightly ajar.

Something was definitely off. I couldn't even sense anyone inside. *Are they all sleeping?* That didn't explain my uneasy feeling, though.

I slipped my shoes off at the door and carried them with me as I crept down the corridor. *I'm a demon, not a thief,* I kept telling myself. I approached the open door as silently as possible and peered inside trepidatiously. I quickly realized the light was coming from a set of candles.

"…Hi there. I'm the demon from the House of Gremory… Did you summon me?" I whispered nervously.

There was no reply. *Guess I have no choice.* I steeled myself and stepped through the door.

It was an ordinary living room, complete with a sofa, a television, and a table. And yet… I caught my breath. My eyes were rooted to the wall. A corpse had been nailed to it upside down.

"…It's human." *A man. Is this his house…?*

The body had been eviscerated. Bloody guts sagged from various wounds. I retched, my stomach churning at the putrid sight. I'd been all right during the battle with the stray demon the other day, but this was on a whole different level. The sight of the corpse was just too much.

Someone had pinned it head down so the body hung in the shape of an inverted cross. The stakes securing the corpse to the wall had been driven through both hands, both legs, and the center of the chest.

This is messed up! No sane person would kill someone this way!

The floor was covered in pools of blood, with even more of the dark-red liquid streaking the walls. There was a message next to the body, written in what looked to be the victim's blood.

"Wh-what the…?"

"Punish the wicked. Words to live by. Wise advice from a holy man." All of a sudden, a voice sounded from the shadows behind me.

I spun around to find a white-haired youth. He looked like he was from overseas and in his late teens. The guy was dressed like a priest—and wouldn't you know it, he was a total pretty boy, too. As soon as he laid eyes on me, he broke into a sinister grin.

"Well, well, well, if it isn't a puny little demon." He sneered, looking pretty pleased with himself.

Rias's warning from the other day suddenly echoed in my mind. *"Don't involve yourself with anyone even remotely connected to the Church. Exorcists, in particular, are our mortal enemies. They carry God's blessing and are capable of destroying us at will."*

If he was a priest, that meant he was definitely connected to the Church. *This is bad…* To top it off, he knew I was a demon. Could my situation have been any worse?

Out of nowhere, the pretty boy broke into a freaky song: *"Yes, I'm a priest, a youthful priest, here to slay this demon beast! With a grin and a laugh, I'll tear you in half, and have me a glorious feast!"*

Wh-what the hell?! What's wrong with this guy?!

"Freed Sellzen, at your service. I work for a certain devil-purging organization you may have heard of. Ah, don't feel obliged to introduce yourself just because I did. I don't really care who you are. Fret not, you will perish soon! I will make sure of that. It may be painful at first, but you'll be crying for joy before too long. Now let's get a move on!"

I'd never met a man like this before. His words and behavior were inexplicable, but it sure seemed like he was an exorcist. I was in trouble now. Nonetheless, there was something I had to know. I swallowed my breath.

"Hey, was it you? Did you kill this guy?"

"Yes, yes, this is my handiwork. Summoning you was proof of his wickedness. I had to kill him."

Wh-what the hell?!

"Oh? Surprised? You aren't going to turn tail? You're a strange one. *Very* strange. Only the lowest of the low would deal with contemptible demons like yourself. Degenerate scum! Do you understand what I'm saying? No? I guess not. You *are* a wretched demon, after all."

There was no point talking with this prick! I never stood a chance of getting through to him but still wanted to say my piece. "How can you kill a fellow human being?! Aren't you supposed to destroy demons?!"

"What? *You*, a lowly demon, presume to lecture *me*? How ludicrous! I owe you a commendation for your sense of humor. Listen up, *demon*. Your kind thrives on the base desires of humans like this. Summoning the likes of you was proof that he was done being human. Game over. End of the road. So I finished him off. Now heed this: Putting down degenerate demons and the lost souls who would cry out to them is my life's work!"

"N-not even a demon would go this far!"

"Come again? What're you saying? Demon scum. Isn't it obvious? Or are you that stupid? Maybe you should go back to basics and try things over in the next life...? Ah, I don't know why I'm wasting my time on reincarnated slime like you. Allow me to expunge you from this world! Ha-ha!" The priest reached into his pocket, pulling out a bladeless hilt and a gun. An electric vibration buzzed through the air as a burning light erupted from the hilt.

What the...? It's like a beam weapon from Dungam.

"Can I butcher you? Can I shoot you? You're fine with that, right? Very well. First, I'm going to cut out your evil heart with my heavenly blade of light, then I'm going to blow a hole in your wicked demon face! How does that sound?!" The priest came charging toward me, lashing out with his sword.

Wha—?! I managed to tumble away from the slash, but an intense pain coursed through my leg. Smoke was rising from the barrel of the priest's gun. *Did he shoot me?!* I hadn't heard any gunshots. Out of nowhere, another bolt of agony ran through my other leg.

"Gah!" I moaned, falling to my knees. This time, it was my left leg the priest had hit. Damn, it really hurt.

"How's that? Light-based bullets—the ammunition of choice for exorcists! They don't even make a sound. Because they're made of light, get it? What a *thrilling* situation, wouldn't you say, demon?"

That explained the pain. Light was poison for us demons. The faintest scratch was enough to bring pure agony.

"Die, demon, die! Perish! I'll reduce you to ashes on the wind! Heh, I'm going to enjoy this!" The priest laughed madly as he moved to finish me off.

"Stop!" Interrupting the chaos came a familiar voice. The priest froze in place, weapons poised above me, and glanced toward the source of the disruption. My gaze, too, was drawn in that direction...

It's her!

"Asia," muttered the priest.

It was true. The voice that had paused our fight belonged to the nun I'd met the other day.

"Well, if it isn't my assistant. What are you doing? Have you finished setting up the barrier already?"

"Ahhhhhh!" she shrieked when she noticed the corpse hanging on the wall.

"What an adorable little scream! Right, this is your first time seeing a body, isn't it? In that case, look carefully. This is what the job entails, my dear. We dispose of unfortunate people who have been bewitched by the evil demons."

"...Th-that's..." When Asia eventually brought herself to look away and turn toward me, her eyes opened wide in shock.

"...Father Freed... This man..." Her words tapered off. Asia's gaze was fixed on me.

"Man? No, no, no. This is a lowly demon. Ha-ha, looks can be deceiving, you know."

"...Issei...is a demon...?" She seemed so taken aback that Asia was at a loss for what to say next.

"Oh? You know him? Now *this* is a surprise! Forbidden love between a demon and a sister? You must be kidding me!" The priest—Freed—looked back and forth between the two of us with amusement.

...I hadn't wanted her to learn the truth. Things should have stayed the way they were between us. Back then, I'd thought it would've been better if Asia didn't know what I was. I'd never planned on seeing her again. All I wanted was for her to think of me as a kind, local high schooler.

Why did it have to come to this? What cruel fate. The pain in her eyes made me feel somehow guilty. *I'm sorry. I'm sorry for being a demon.*

"Ha! Demons and humanity can never coexist! Their kind and the Church are mortal enemies! You realize we are a band of heretics forsaken by God, right? Neither you nor I could survive without the support and protection of the fallen angels."

Fallen angels? What's he talking about? Don't he and Asia work for the Church?

"Well, putting that aside, my job isn't finished if I don't butcher this scum, so here goes. Ready yourself." The priest aimed his sword of light for my chest.

If he followed through, I'd probably die on the spot... Even if I didn't, that priest would just nail me to the wall and slice me into pieces like he did my client.

Fear took hold of my body just thinking about it. *At this rate, I'm screwed!* Unable even to move, I saw nothing but death ahead of me! However, to my surprise, Asia inserted herself between the priest and me. She stood over me, her arms outstretched as if to shield me.

The priest's expression turned sour. "...Come on, are you serious? Asia, do you realize what you're doing?"

"...Yes. Father Freed, please. Forgive him. Let him go."

Her words left me speechless. *Asia? Are you really willing to protect me?*

"I can't stand this... You can't kill people just because they might have been beguiled by a demon, and you can't kill demons for no reason. It's wrong!"

"Haaaaaaaaaah?! What are you saying, you dumb nun?! Hasn't the Church taught you what these things *are*? Have you lost your mind?!" Freed's expression was indignant.

"Even among demons, there are good people!"

"As if!"

"I—I believed that once... But Issei is a good person! Being a demon doesn't change that! And murder is unforgivable! The Lord won't permit it!" Even after discovering that corpse, even after learning my true nature, Asia was still brave enough to stand up for what she believed in.

She was strong-willed, that was for sure. It was amazing.

Thud!

"Kyah!"

That messed-up priest struck Asia on the head with the side of his gun, sending her sprawling onto the floor.

"Asia!" I called out, diving after her. There was a dark bruise on her face. The bastard had actually hit her.

"...That fallen angel told me in no uncertain terms that I wasn't to kill you, but I've had it up to here! If I can't end your miserable life, maybe I'll just desecrate your flesh? I'll need to have a little fun with you if I'm going to heal my wounded heart. But first things first. I need to erase that piece of scum over there." The priest pointed his glowing sword at me again.

I couldn't run away if it meant leaving Asia here. Definitely not after what he had suggested doing to her! If I was going to escape, I had to bring her with me. Which meant I would have to fight. Could I use the Sacred Gear in combat? I didn't even really know what it was capable of. Did a Pawn, the weakest of the weak, really stand a chance? No matter the odds, I had to do something…

"I'm not about to abandon a woman who came to my protection. Come get me!" I cried, readying myself in a fighting pose.

The priest let out an amused whistle. "Huh? Huh? Seriously? *Seriously?* You want to fight *me*? Do you have a death wish? Do you *want* to suffer? I'm not going to make it quick. You realize that? All right then, what say we aim for a new world record, demon scum? Let's see how many pieces of meat I can chop you into!"

Man, he really said some deranged stuff. *Ha-ha… I guess this is it for me, then?* Even if it was, I had to put up a good fight if Asia was watching!

The priest prepared to leap into the air—and at that moment, the floor erupted in a bluish-white glow.

"What the—?!" The priest stared down at his feet in confusion as the light gradually took on a familiar form.

It was a magic circle—and not just any magic circle. As it materialized, it took on the unmistakable shape of the Gremory Familia crest!

Flash!

There was a brilliant burst of light as four recognizable figures stepped forward.

"We're here to rescue you, Hyoudou," Kiba declared with a bold grin.

"Oh dear, aren't we in a spot of trouble?"

"…A priest."

Akeno and Koneko had come, too! My allies had swooped in to help me! I was so touched, I felt like I could've burst into tears! Incredible! I never would've expected a last-second rescue.

"Oh? A whole band of demons!" Unconcerned by their sudden appearance, the priest brought his sword down on me.

Clang!

A metallic sound reverberated through the room. Kiba had blocked the priest's attack with his own blade.

"Sorry, but he's one of us! I won't let you harm him!"

"Oh, what touching camaraderie for a demon! So what's this, you guys on your way to a game show already? Are you the Devil Rangers? I can feel the heat already! Tell me, what's your deal? You're the pitcher, and he's the catcher?" The priest stuck out his tongue as he exchanged blows with Kiba.

He was mocking us! Even Kiba was clearly disgusted.

"…For a priest, that's quite a mouth you've got there… You must be what they call a 'stray exorcist.'"

"Oh, I'm so *sorry*! It's not like I asked them to kick me out! Screw the Vatican! But enough about them! Right now, hunting your kind is my only concern!"

The two were locked in combat, each parrying the other's attacks. Kiba's expression was as composed as ever, but his eyes were filled with unwavering focus. On the other hand, the priest—Freed— continued laughing maniacally.

"People like you are such a pain. Your only pleasure comes from hunting demons… There's nothing more dangerous to us than your kind."

"Hah? Another preaching demon? I'm just trying to live my life as best I can! Why should I let vermin like *you* talk down to *me*?!"

"Even demons live by rules," Akeno interjected. Her lips were curled in a faint smile, but her gaze was unyielding. I could sense her rising anger and lust for destruction.

"Oh, what sultry eyes! You're killing me! Is this love? No? Murderous intent? I could eat you up!"

"I think that's about enough."

Out of nowhere, a crimson-haired beauty appeared by my side—Rias!

"I'm sorry, Issei. I never expected a stray exorcist to show up at a client's house." The prez paused there, her eyes narrowing as she realized I was injured. "…Issei, did he hurt you?"

"Ah, sorry… I—I got shot, I guess…" I tried to brush her off with a forced laugh. I was sure she was going to lay into me later. *Sorry for being so weak, Prez.*

Far from scolding me, though, Rias turned her frigid gaze to the priest. "You've been playing with my cute little servant, I take it?" Her voice was almost inaudibly low.

Whoa. Is she angry about what happened to me?

"Oh yes, we've been having quite a time! I was going to carve him into itty-bitty pieces, but now that you're all here, that plan has gone up in smoke!"

Bang! A piece of furniture behind the priest was suddenly engulfed in a powerful blast. The source of the attack was a furious Rias. She had hurled a ball of demonic energy right at the crazy priest.

"I never forgive those who hurt my servants, and I will *never* tolerate a lowlife like you damaging my possessions." The temperature seemed to have plummeted. I could feel Rias's wrath filling the room. Waves of demonic power were reverberating around her.

"—! President, a fallen angel is on its way. We should hurry." Akeno must have sensed someone approaching.

A fallen angel? The ones with the black wings?

Rias glared menacingly at the priest. "…Akeno, we're leaving as soon as we have Issei. Prepare to jump."

"Right." At Rias's urging, Akeno began to intone an incantation.

Jump? We're running away?

I glanced back to Asia. "Prez! We need to take her with us!"

"I'm afraid only demons can use magic circles, and this one is only compatible with members of my Familia."

C-come on...that's some kind of joke, right? My gaze met Asia's. She simply smiled back at me.

"Asia!"

"I'll see you again, Issei," she said in farewell.

Then, with Akeno's spell complete, a glowing magic circle traced itself on the floor again.

"You think I'm going to let you escape?!" The priest came lunging toward us, but Koneko simply hurled a nearby sofa at him. By the time he had presumably pushed it aside with his sword, we'd already teleported away.

My first journey through a magic circle didn't leave a very lasting impression. All I could think about was Asia's parting smile.

—○●○—

"There are two types of exorcists in the world," Rias explained as she treated my legs in the clubroom. "The first are those who act in the name of justice, having received Heaven's blessing. This group borrows on the powers of God and angels to eliminate us demons. And then there's the other kind—stray exorcists."

"Strays?"

Rias nodded in answer. *So there are two kinds of strays...*

"Exorcism is a holy ceremony performed in the name of God. Every now and then, however, there are exorcists who take pleasure in slaying demons. For them, destroying us becomes their sole purpose in life. The Church doesn't tolerate such individuals and either expels them from its ranks or considers them too dangerous and eliminates them."

"Eliminate... You mean they kill them?"

"There are those, however, who manage to survive. And where do they go? They run off to the fallen angels."

"They're the ones with black wings, right?"

"Yes. Fallen angels may have been driven from Heaven, but they still possess the power of light—the power to destroy demons. They, too, lost many allies and most of their manpower in the Great War and so have taken to recruiting servants just as we have."

At last, I finally understood the whole situation.

"So those exorcists who want to kill demons make natural allies to the fallen angels, who see us as obstacles?"

"Precisely. That is why we call them stray exorcists. The fallen angels feed their addiction to slaughter, allowing them free reign to slay demons and the humans who summon them. That young priest was one such individual—a stray exorcist belonging to some organization backed by the fallen angels. They may not be legitimate exorcists, but they are extremely dangerous—more dangerous than true exorcists, in point of fact, as they don't restrain themselves in the ways that their more high-minded brethren do. No good will come from getting involved with them. What's more, we now know that the church you visited, Issei, is dedicated not to God but to the fallen angels."

I knew something was wrong with that place.

After my encounter with that psycho priest, I knew firsthand just how dangerous they were. He was pure evil. All he cared about—the only thing that brought him joy—was fighting and slaughtering demons. It was madness to have anything to do with a group composed of such people. That was clear as day, and yet…

"Prez, what about Asia?" I asked.

"I'm afraid it's impossible. How would you save her? You're a demon, and she serves them. Trying to rescue her would mean making enemies of the fallen angels… If you do that, we will all be forced to fight."

"…" There was nothing I could say to that. I couldn't put Rias and the others in jeopardy. Trying to weigh Asia against Rias and the others revealed no answer. They were all important to me.

That's... That's...

Unable to find a solution, I was painfully reminded just how miserable an existence I was.

I couldn't even save one girl. I was just too weak.

"Hahh."

It was around noon, and I had taken the day off from school. Setting myself down on a bench in a children's park, I let out a tired sigh.

My legs, wounded from the priest's attack the previous day, had yet to fully heal. According to Rias, the priest must have received considerable power from the fallen angels to wield such damaging light. Since light was so toxic to demons, my injuries had been pretty severe. Unable to do any demon work for a while, Rias had instructed me to take some time off. Seeing as she pulled all the strings at Kuou Academy, she'd probably made sure my teachers wouldn't have any problems with my absence.

Grrrrr. My stomach rumbled. *Right, I haven't had anything to eat since morning.* My mind had been caught in a loop, turning over everything with Asia and my life as a demon.

What can I do to help her? Is she even unhappy in her situation? I had no idea. But if I had to guess, it was hard to imagine anyone enjoying working alongside that psycho priest. Especially after he'd struck her.

Hmm... If I act alone, I'd end up causing problems for Rias and the others. That means I have to get stronger. That was what I had to focus on. There were certain things that could only be accomplished through strength. In my short time as a demon, I had learned that many times over already. I wouldn't be able to push forward on this path if I didn't have the strength to take the steps.

Since I'd first called it, I'd learned how to activate my Sacred Gear at will. Still, I had no idea how to use it, so that didn't do me much good. It seemed like a bad idea to rely solely on that anyway.

All right, once my wounds are healed, I'm gonna start working out! Plus, I'll ask Rias and Akeno to teach me how to use my powers! As much as it pained me to do so, I even considered asking Kiba to teach me how to use a sword. In any event, my next step was clear.

I would become stronger than that psycho priest—strong enough to escape a fallen angel on my own. I might be a Pawn, but with ambition and persistence, I knew I could do it. At least, I *believed* I could do it. With my plan formulated, it was time to go home and get some lunch!

However, the second I rose from the bench, a flash of golden-yellow appeared in the corner of my eye. With a gasp, I turned around to find a familiar, blond beauty standing before me. She clearly recognized me, too. The two of us stood there, stunned in mute shock for a moment.

"…Asia?"

"…Issei?"

—○●○—

"Um…"

It was an unusual sight—a nun frozen in bewilderment in front of the cash register at a fast-food restaurant.

"Er, your order…" The clerk clearly didn't know how to handle this situation, either.

I'd taken Asia to a restaurant downtown for lunch. Apparently, this was her first time coming to a place like this, and she was struggling to make her order. I'd offered to help, but she insisted she could manage, and as I didn't want to dampen her spirits, I decided to watch from the sidelines, despite the fact that she still couldn't speak Japanese…

Unable to stand by any longer, I moved to help her. "Sorry. She'll have the same as me."

"All right, then," the clerk answered, taking our orders.

Asia, however, was despondent. "I can't even buy a hamburger by myself..."

"W-well, let's focus on improving your Japanese first," I said trying to encourage her as we took an empty table.

Most of the other male customers stared at Asia as we moved through the restaurant.

Part of it was no doubt because she was a nun, a rare sight in and of itself, but her intense level of cuteness was likely a factor, too. I mean, how could any guy have brought himself to turn away from her?

Asia and I sat across from each other. We had both ordered regular hamburger meal sets, but Asia merely stared at her food pensively.

Maybe she doesn't know how to eat it? I wondered. *Talk about a hack-neyed scenario.*

"You take off the wrapper slightly, like this, my lady," I said with a grin before raising the burger to my mouth.

"S-so that's how you do it! Here goes!"

What an adorable reaction. She sure is cute.

"Then you grab the fries like this."

"Oh my!" Asia watched intently.

"N-now you try."

"R-right..." She took a small bite out of her burger. Nibble by nibble, she began making her way through the food. "Th-this is delicious!" she exclaimed, her eyes gleaming.

"Haven't you ever had a hamburger before?"

"No. I've seen them on television, but this is my first time eating one. I'm impressed! It's so tasty!"

"Oh? What do you usually eat?"

"Bread and soup, mostly. And vegetables and pasta."

How plain, I thought. *Is it like that for everyone in the Church?*

"I see, I see. Well then, I'm glad you like it."

"Yes, it's wonderful." She really did seem to be enjoying herself as she pecked away at her meal.

My mind drifted back to wondering what Asia had been doing in the park. She'd said she'd been given a break, but no matter how you looked at it, she'd seemed afraid. Almost as if something was after her. The moment Asia had seen me, it was as if a wave of relief had washed over her face.

I wanted to ask what was troubling her but didn't want to make things uncomfortable between us. It was better to let her be the one to broach the topic. Regardless, no matter the problem, I'd already made up my mind to help her. I did have Rias and the others to worry about, too, but I couldn't tell Asia about them. I wished I could have. Truly, I did.

Anyway, given how much she was enjoying her hamburger, I didn't want to say anything to spoil the mood.

Hey, that's it! We should just forget about everything for a while! With that, I made my decision.

"Asia."

"Y-yes?"

"Let's have some fun today."

"Huh?"

"Next stop, the arcade!"

"The Legendary Downhill Night Driver, Issei!"

Vrooooom! I slammed my foot down on the accelerator and rapidly switched gears as the car swung around the corner. In a split second, I had whipped past both of the cars ahead of me!

"Y-you're so fast, Issei!"

Heh-heh, are you watching, Asia? Now, fall in love with my expert handling! The two of us were playing a racing game at the local arcade.

The truth is, before joining the Occult Research Club, I hadn't belonged to any after-school activities. Matsuda, Motohama, and I would often run off to the nearby arcades for a bit of fun. No matter the game, nothing could stand in the way of my victory!

You win! flashed the message on the screen, announcing my

triumph. *A new record...* I was drunk on my own success. Only then did I realize that Asia had vanished. I scanned my surroundings, finding her standing in front of a claw machine.

"What is it?" I asked.

"Ah! N-no... N-nothing!" she answered, dodging the question.

"There's something you want, isn't there?" The machine was filled with toys of Ratchu, a cute mascot character based on a mouse.

Right, Ratchu may have been created in Japan, but it's popular worldwide. That's probably why she recognized it.

"You like Ratchu, don't you?" I asked.

"Huh?! N-no, I mean..." Her cheeks turned red in embarrassment, but she gave me a quick nod.

"All right then, I'll get you one."

"Huh?! B-but...!"

"Leave it to me."

I had to strike while the iron was hot! I put a coin into the machine and started the crane game. Maybe I'm outing myself here, but I'm pretty good at these manual, skill-based kind of games. Or so I thought. I was actually having a hard time winning anything.

My initial attempt looked like it was going well at first, but then I let the toy slip. On my second go, I messed it up completely. The third and fourth attempts were no good, either, but just as Asia appeared to have given up hope...I snagged the toy on my fifth try.

"Yeah!" I pumped my fist, retrieved the stuffed animal from drop slot, and handed it to the blond nun. "Here you go, Asia."

The girl looked truly overjoyed as she hugged the plush character close to her chest. "Thank you, Issei. I'll treasure it."

"If you love Ratchu that much, I'll get you another one."

Asia shook her head. "No, I'll keep this one as a memory of today. I'm so happy I bumped into you. I've had a wonderful time. I'll cherish this Ratchu forever."

It was a pretty embarrassing thing to hear, yet coming from her, those words filled me with bliss. Still, the day was young!

"All right! We've only just started! Asia, we're really gonna have some fun today—come on!"

"O-okay!"

I took her hand and led her further into the arcade.

—○●○—

"Ahhh, I think we may have overdone it!"

"Y-yes… I *am* a little tired…"

We both broke into exhausted laughter as we made our way down the street. By the time we'd stopped, it was already evening. I'd ended up skipping an entire day of school and spent the whole time having fun instead.

We were lucky that neither of us had bumped into a police officer. They probably would've insisted on taking us to a train station to make sure we went to class.

Though the day had been exacting, not once had I grown tired of watching Asia's refreshingly innocent reaction to the arcade games and the various shops we perused. All the planning I'd done in preparation for my date with Yuuma had actually come in handy. I guess you never know what life is going to throw at you next.

"Ngh…" I almost tripped as a strange feeling, followed by a weak pain, ran up my leg. "Ouch…" It was my injury from the day before, specifically, the spot where the psycho priest had shot me. Looked like it still needed some time to heal.

"…Issei, are you all right? Don't tell me, what happened yesterday…" Asia's expression clouded over.

Damn, I messed up, I thought. We'd been having so much fun, and now I had ruined the mood by reminding her of something we both would have rather forgotten.

Nonetheless, Asia leaned over to inspect my injury. "Can I take a look?" she asked.

"Uh, sure…"

Asia lifted the hem of my pant leg, exposing my left calf. The gunshot wound was clearly visible. She placed her hand on it, and a warm, gentle light coursed through my flesh. It was a truly heart-warming glow that was green in hue—the same beautiful color as Asia's eyes. I could feel her innate kindness flowing through me.

"How is it now?" she asked as the glow faded.

I tried moving my leg slightly. *Whoa, amazing!* "Incredible, Asia! It doesn't hurt at all! It's completely healed!" She smiled happily as she watched me take off in an exaggerated run. "You're amazing, Asia! That healing power you have—it's incredible... It's from a Sacred Gear, right?"

"Yes."

So I was right, I thought.

"To tell you the truth, I've got a Sacred Gear, too. Although, it doesn't do much. Not yet anyway."

Asia opened her eyes wide in surprise at my confession. "You have one, too? I didn't realize..."

"Ah, well, I don't even know what it's capable of yet. But yours is amazing, Asia. You can heal humans, animals, and even demons like me, right?"

Despite my words, Asia's expression was troubled, and she bowed her head. After a short moment, a solitary teardrop fell from her cheek. Before I knew it, that single tear had turned into a flood, and the girl broke down weeping. I didn't know what to do, so I brought her to a bench to sit down. Then, she began to explain her fate as a Holy Maiden.

When Asia was a baby, she'd been abandoned by her parents. They'd left her at a church in a small European town. There, she'd been brought up along with other orphans by a convent of nuns. From her earliest memories, Asia had been raised with a deep sense of spirituality. Then, when she was eight years old, she'd been blessed with a special power.

Asia had come across a badly injured puppy and, through some mysterious gift, healed its wounds. A member of the Catholic Church happened to witness this miracle, and from that moment onward, Asia's life changed completely.

The young girl was taken to the Vatican, where she came to be seen as a living saint, a Holy Maiden. Worshippers flocked to Asia for her blessing, praying she could heal their ailments. Rumor spread, and Asia found herself being revered by the Church's many adherents, regardless of the blond girl's own wishes.

Still, Asia didn't complain about the way she was treated. The people from the Church were good to her, and she didn't think it was right to blame the sick and injured. Asia was just happy that she could use her power to benefit others. The young nun was thankful to God for bestowing it upon her. Nevertheless, she was lonely.

The girl didn't have any friends to whom she could bare her heart. Everyone around Asia treated her kindly and with respect, but none of them considered her a friend. The reason was easy enough to understand.

Asia knew that when they looked at her, what they saw was an inhuman power. To everyone else, she was an entity capable of healing, but she wasn't a *person*. Then, one day, change visited the young nun once again.

Completely by chance, she had stumbled upon an injured demon and healed its wounds. After all, she wasn't the type to ignore someone's suffering, demon or not. She had a responsibility to do what she could. It was her innate kindness that drove her to action. However, that decision threw her life upside down. Someone from the Church must have witnessed what she'd done and notified the clergy, who were furious.

"A power that heals demons?!"

"This is intolerable!"

"The Lord's blessing should only bring deliverance to true believers!"

Yes, there were those throughout the world with the ability to heal others, but someone who could heal demons—that was unheard of.

Up until then, the Church had assumed Asia's skills couldn't possibly have been effective when on demons or fallen angels.

There had been people like her once, a long time ago. In ancient days, there were those with the dreaded power to heal demons and fallen angels—witches. Thus, the clergy declared Asia a heretic.

"Demon-worshipping witch!"

The girl, once revered as a Holy Maiden, was now feared and reviled as a witch, all because her ability could be used to heal demons as well as the faithful. The Catholic Church threw her out without a second thought.

With nowhere to turn and no place to go, Asia found herself recruited by an organization of stray exorcists. In other words, she had no choice but to accept the protection of fallen angels.

Nonetheless, she never forgot to pray to God or offer Him thanks.

Despite her plights, however, she'd been abandoned. God didn't help her. The greatest shock of all had been that no one in the Church, not one person, had been willing to stand up for her. Asia was alone.

"...My prayers weren't enough. I'm sure of it. Look at me; I'm so clumsy, so incompetent. I couldn't even order a hamburger by myself..." The blond nun wiped away her tears as she let out a forced laugh.

I didn't know how to answer. I had no clue how to respond after hearing about her devastating past. As she'd demonstrated just moments before, she possessed a Sacred Gear that allowed her to cure the wounds of anyone, even demons.

"The Lord is testing me. I'm a bad nun, so he's putting me through these trials to teach me. I have to endure them." She let out a weak laugh, as if trying to convince herself.

There's no need to go on, Asia. I understand..., I thought, unable to get the words out.

"I'll make lots of friends one day; I'm sure of it. I have a dream, you know? I'll go and buy flowers with my friends, and read books...and talk..." She paused there, choking on her tears.

I couldn't bear to watch in silence anymore. Asia had been suffering alone all this time. She'd been burying her true feelings for so long, waiting for God to save her.

Hey you, God! What the heck are you playing at?! Why won't you do anything for her?! She's been calling out for you all this time! She respects you more than anyone else! So why won't you help her?! Why won't you do anything?!

I might not know anything about you, and I've certainly never prayed before. To top things off, I'm a demon. But even as a demon, I can still reach out to help her! Weren't you the one who gave us these Sacred Gears in the first place?! That's it! Fine! Watch this, God!

I took Asia's hand in my own, gazed directly into her teary eyes, and said: "Asia, I'll be your friend. I mean, we're already friends."

She stared back at me blankly.

"Ah, I might be a demon, but it's okay. I won't take your life, and I won't exact payment! Call me whenever you feel like it! Ah! I'll give you my phone number." I reached into my pocket to retrieve my cell phone.

"…But why?"

"Why do you think? We've spent the whole day having fun together, right? And we talked? And laughed? Then that settles it—we're friends! Demons, humans, God—none of that matters! You and I are friends!"

"…Is this a pact with a demon?"

"No! We're real-life friends! Nothing else matters! We'll talk when we want to, have fun when we want to, and… Right, let's go shopping together next time! Books or flowers, whatever you're interested in! All right?" Even I could hear how awkward I sounded. *So much for building a romantic atmosphere.* Kiba would've probably been much suaver about it.

Regardless of my stammering, Asia raised her hand to her face and broke down in tears once again. This time, however, it wasn't out of sadness.

"…Issei… I don't know anything about the world."

"Then I'll take you around town! I'll show you all kinds of things!"

"...I can't even speak Japanese. And I don't know anything about the culture..."

"I'll teach you! I'll have you reciting proverbs in no time! Just leave it to me! I'll introduce you to the culture as well! Samurai! Sushi! Geisha! You name it!"

"...And I don't know what I'm supposed to say to a friend..."

I tightened my grip on Asia's hand. "We've spent the whole day talking. It's like we've already been friends forever. That's all we need."

"...You'll really be my friend?"

"Yep, I'll be here for you whenever you need me, Asia."

Her teary face finally broke out into a smile as she gave me a warm nod, and I knew everything would be fine. She and I were friends! No matter how much this situation made me blush... That night, when I went to bed, I knew I'd probably get embarrassed recalling this conversation. Even so, I didn't care. I'd made Asia smile, and that was worth a little awkwardness.

I might not have been able to truly appreciate the hardships she'd endured, but I was determined to make sure her future was bright! What was really stopping a demon from befriending a nun anyway? No matter how impossible I'd thought it would be at first, all that seemed unimportant after our day together. From then on, she was my friend, and I wouldn't let anyone stand between us. I would protect her!

"Impossible," interrupted a new voice, almost as if responding to my thoughts.

When I saw who had called out to us, I swallowed in trepidation. I knew that face—just as I knew that slender-bodied young woman with jet-black hair. It was Yuuma Amano.

"Y-Yuuma...?" I murmured in disbelief.

She let out a little chuckle. "Oh? You're alive? And a demon now, too? You poor thing." Yuuma spoke not with the cute tone of a high school girl but with the rich sultriness of a lascivious adult.

"...Mistress Raynare...," Asia said softly.

Raynare? Ah right. I'd almost forgot. Yuuma Amano was a fallen angel. Raynare must have been her real name.

"...What do you want?" I called out to her.

"Don't talk to me like that, you filthy, low-level demon," she sneered back. Raynare narrowed her eyes contemptuously, as if she found me truly revolting. "That girl, Asia—she belongs to me. Return her at once. And you, Asia—you should have known better than to run away."

Run away? What is she talking about?

"...No. I don't want to go back to that church. I don't want to kill people... A-and you all...to me..." Asia's flat rejection seemed to hide something more. Hatred, perhaps? What exactly had happened to her at that old chapel?

"Don't say that, Asia. Your Sacred Gear is essential to our plans. So how about you just come back with me? I went out of my way to find you, you know? Don't cause me any more trouble." Raynare began slowly approaching us.

Asia hid behind me. Her whole body was trembling with fear. I stepped forward to shield her.

"Wait. Can't you see she doesn't want to go with you? Yuuma—no, Raynare—what do you want with her?"

"How dare you sully my name! This has nothing to do with you. Scurry off to your master now. Or would you prefer I kill you?"

A pillar of light began coalescing in Raynare's hand. *A spear?* She'd already killed me once that way. I had to make the first move!

"S-Sacred Gear!" I cried out to the heavens, and a red light suddenly enveloped my left arm, taking the form of an elbow-length gauntlet.

All right! All that practice paid off!

No sooner did Raynare set her eyes on my Sacred Gear, however, than she snorted derisively. "Word upstairs is you're a demon to watch out for, a force to be reckoned with. How wrong they were!" She looked truly amused with this development.

What's so funny? I wondered.

"What a basic Sacred Gear. That's nothing more than a Twice Critical. All it does is temporarily double your power, but twice nothing is still nothing. Truly a fitting weapon for a useless, low-grade demon like yourself."

The ability to double my innate power? That's what my Sacred Gear does? And it's common? Whatever, it's good enough. It has to be. Before anything else, though, I needed to find a way to escape with Asia and lose Raynare.

Where could we go? The school? No, I don't want to cause any more trouble for Rias. Home? But how would I explain this to my parents? Damn... What good am I as a friend if I can't even think of somewhere safe to take her?!

This was no time to be feeling sorry for myself! First things first; I had to defeat this fallen angel! Seriously, though, why did it have to be my ex-girlfriend?! This is the kind of absurd stuff that would only happen to someone like me.

"Sacred Gear! Activate! Double my power! Show me what you're made of!" The jewel embedded on the back of the gauntlet began glowing at my words.

"Boost!" A powerful voice boomed from my hand, and a wave of energy flowed through me. *Is this how it works? All right! With this—*

Stab. There was a dull, thick sound. Something had skewered me through my stomach.

It was Raynare's spear of light. She'd impaled me. Again.

"Even after increasing your power, you can't even dodge one measly spear. Someone like you can't hold a candle to me. Do you get it now, lowly demon?"

I collapsed to the ground. This was bad. Light was poison to demons, and it had passed right through my stomach... I steeled myself for the torment and death that was sure to follow, but there was no pain. Instead, a soft, green light had engulfed my body.

When I looked up, Asia was healing me. She had placed her hand on my abdomen and was mending my wound. The spear embedded inside me grew smaller and smaller until it disappeared entirely. I didn't feel even a tinge of pain—only Asia's warmth.

"Asia. Unless you want me to kill this demon, you had better come with me. We need your Sacred Gear. Your power, Twilight Healing, is much rarer and infinitely more valuable than his could ever be. If you won't submit, I'll have no choice but to kill him."

Hold on, I'm the leverage?! "S-screw you! There's no way—"

"I understand," Asia interrupted, accepting the fallen angel's ultimatum.

"Asia!"

"Issei. Thank you so much for today. I had fun." The blond nun gave me the widest smile she could manage. Having completely healed me, Asia walked toward the fallen angel, taking one last look at me.

"That's a good girl, Asia. There's no need to worry. After the ritual tonight, all your pain and suffering will be over." Raynare broke into a cruel grin.

Dammit! This fallen angel doesn't look a thing like the Yuuma I know! And what was that about a ritual? Doesn't everyone know stuff like that sounds totally evil? "Asia, wait!" I cried. "We're friends—remember that!"

"I know. Thank you for spending time with someone like me."

No matter what, I wasn't about to give up on my promise to protect her. "Asia, I'll come for you!"

A warm expression spread across the nun's face. I stood transfixed by her for a moment, until—

"Good-bye," she said with an air of finality. Then Raynare enveloped her in those black wings.

"I'll spare you this time, lowly demon. You can thank this girl for that. The next time you get in my way, though, I really will kill you. Until then, Issei." The fallen angel sneered one final time before ascending high into the air, Asia in tow. The next thing I knew, both of them had disappeared.

I was left alone with a few fluttering, black feathers and Asia's stuffed Ratchu toy, which was lying on the ground where it had fallen. I hadn't been able to do anything.

So much for protecting her... I fell to my knees and slammed my fist hard into the asphalt. Again and again, I pounded, grinding my teeth in desperation as tears of anguish rolled down my cheeks.

Dammit. Dammit. Dammit! "Asia...," I called out to the empty sky, but there was no response. "Asiaaaaa!"

For the first time in my life, I cursed my pathetic weakness.

Life.4
I'm Saving My Friend!

Thwack!

The dry sound of Rias slapping my cheek with the flat of her hand echoed throughout the clubroom. Her expression was deathly serious. "How many times must I repeat myself? No means no. I won't allow it."

Unable to help Asia alone, I'd made my way back to the school and told Rias what had happened. Then, after explaining the situation, I suggested we go to the church. My goal was to rescue Asia, of course.

Rias, however, was adamant that none of us should get involved. Unable to accept her decision, I'd kept insisting. That was when she hit me. It was the first time in my life someone had slapped me, but my heart hurt more than my face. It seemed I was destined to keep betraying Rias's expectations of me, but I wasn't going to give up on Asia.

"I'll go myself, then. I'm worried about this ritual thing. If the fallen angels are involved, it can't be good. There's no guarantee they won't harm Asia."

"Don't be foolish," Rias scolded. "If you go there, they'll kill you. You realize there is no coming back next time, right?" The prez was evidently struggling to keep her cool. "Your actions have consequences for me and every one of us here. You are a member of the Gremory Familia! Remember that!"

"In that case, release me from your service! I'll go by myself!"

"Impossible! Why can't you understand?!" I had never seen Rias so enraged before.

Yep, all I do is cause problems for her... I'm sorry, Prez. But I can't quit. After all...

"Asia Argento is my friend. She's important to me. I can't just abandon her!"

"...A noble sentiment. I'm impressed you feel confident enough to say that to my face, but it's beside the point. Relations between demons and fallen angels aren't that simple. Our two sides have been mortally opposed for hundreds, thousands of years. If we show any weakness—any at all—they will slaughter us. They are our enemies."

"I thought the Gremory Familia destroyed its enemies?"

"......"

Rias and I exchanged furious glares. I refused to turn away, keeping my gaze locked on hers.

"That girl was originally affiliated with God and Heaven. She cannot coexist with us. Even now that she's joined the fallen angels, that doesn't change the fact that she is our natural adversary."

"Asia isn't our enemy!" I insisted. After all, how could someone so kind and gentle hate us?

"Even if you were right, she has nothing to do with us. Issei, forget about her."

No matter what Rias said, there was no way I was going to forget Asia that easily. Then Akeno stepped forward and whispered something in Rias's ear.

I wondered what it was. Had something happened? Akeno's expression was serious, but it seemed unrelated to our present discussion. Rias's visage darkened as she listened to Akeno's report. Yep, something was definitely up.

"I have urgent business to attend to. Akeno and I will be away for a short while."

"P-Prez, we haven't finished—"

She raised a finger to her lips, silencing me. "Issei, there are certain things you should know. Firstly, you are under the impression that the Pawn is the weakest chess piece, am I right?"

I nodded silently in response to the question.

"You are mistaken. Pawns have a unique ability that no other pieces possess: *Promotion.*"

Promotion? What's that supposed to be?

"Just as in the actual game of chess, a Pawn can change into any other class once it advances deep enough into the opposing side's territory. Issei, once you reach what I have determined to be the enemy's lines, you will be capable of changing into any other class. That is, with the exception of the King."

I couldn't believe what I was hearing! I could be promoted to a Knight like Kiba, or a Rook like Koneko, or even a Queen like Akeno?!

"You haven't been a demon for very long yet, so there are limitations. You probably won't be able to be promoted to the strongest class, a Queen, just yet. But you could become any of the others. If you dedicate yourself, you should be able to acquire the abilities of any other class."

Incredible! Things were finally turning my way! I reasoned that if I found a method to combine that ability with my Sacred Gear, even that psycho priest wouldn't be able to beat me!

"Another thing. Regarding your Sacred Gear. Issei, keep this in mind when you use it—" Rias began stroking my cheek with her finger. "—Just feel. Sacred Gears are driven by your feelings. That goes for their overall power as well. Emotions are precious, even to demons. The stronger they are, the more powerful your Sacred Gear will become."

My feelings...are what power my Sacred Gear...? In that case, if I want something strongly enough, it should activate for me, right?

"A final piece of advice, Issei: Even a Pawn can capture a King. Just like in chess, so, too, does that apply for us. You are stronger than you think." On that note, Rias and Akeno leaped through the magic circle. Only Kiba, Koneko, and I remained. I let out a deep sigh, gathering my determination.

"Hyoudou," Kiba called out as I turned to leave the room. "Are you still going?"

"Yep. I have to. Asia is my friend. I have to rescue her."

"...They'll kill you. Even with your Sacred Gear, even if you use a Promotion, you can't fight all those exorcists and the fallen angel alone."

Naturally. I was acutely aware of that. "I'm still going. Even if it costs me my life, I'll save Asia."

"I would praise your courage, but it's still a stupid thing to do."

"What other option do I have?!" I shouted back.

Kiba, however, merely answered: "I'm going with you."

"Wha—?" I swallowed my words, taken aback by Kiba's unexpected announcement. Who wouldn't have been surprised? I hadn't seen that one coming.

"I don't know anything about Asia, but you're one of us. No matter what the president says, there's a part of me that respects your resolve. And speaking personally, I don't much care for fallen angels or their priests. I despise them, actually." Kiba's words suggested some sort of history with fallen angels, and to hear him say he considered me his ally...

"You heard what the president said about the fallen angels and about what you're capable of once you reach the enemy lines. She basically said that if you step in that church, you're Promoted."

"Ah..." Only then did I realize that was what Rias had meant. That was why she'd told me how to use my Promotion ability.

"She was indirectly giving you permission to go. Of course, she also said you wouldn't be able to do it on your own. I'm sure she was suggesting that I help you. Otherwise, she would've locked you up somewhere to stop you," Kiba explained with a wry grin.

Thanks, Prez! Once more, I was touched by her generosity. When we were finished saving Asia, I was gonna throw myself into my demon work! A small figure approached me as I mentally thanked my boss.

"...Me, too."

"Wha—?! Koneko?!"

"...Two isn't enough."

Koneko! I'd no idea what was going on behind that expressionless face of hers, but in that moment, I felt like I had brushed against her gentle heart!

"Th-thank you! I'm touched, Koneko!" I found myself getting emotional.

"H-huh? I'm going, too, though..." Kiba sulked.

I was grateful to Kiba, too, of course. He might have been a popular pretty boy, but he could be kind of cute every now and then.

All right! We can do this! "Let's rescue Asia, the three of us!"

Our mission clear, we set out to the church together.

—o●o—

It was growing dark outside as the time the streetlights usually came neared. The three of us—Kiba, Koneko, and myself—were watching the church from a distance. There had been no sign of anyone entering or leaving. Nonetheless, the closer we got to the place, the greater my unease grew. I was practically drenched in my own nervous sweat. According to Kiba, this sensation was proof there was a fallen angel nearby.

Right, so the enemy boss must be inside, I thought.

"Take a look," Kiba said as he spread out what appeared to be a set of blueprints outlining the church.

Where on earth did he get these...?

"I thought knowing the layout would come in handy whenever we needed to attack the enemy base," he said with a charming grin.

Whoa, talk about a perfect follow-through. I'd been planning on barging in without any preparation at all. I was reminded once more just how naive I was.

"In addition to the main hall, there's also a dormitory. It's the nave we should be worrying about." Kiba pointed to an area on the map.

"So we can ignore the dormitory?"

"Probably. Groups of stray exorcists always end up making some sort of alteration to the nave, especially when they want to carry out arcane rituals. Usually in the form of a basement or an underground chamber."

"Why?" I asked.

Kiba flashed me a forced smile. "To avenge themselves by performing acts of blasphemy in what used to be a holy place. They feel abandoned by the God they used to worship, so they choose to defile the holiest part of the building."

They really are messed up, these stray exorcists. Or maybe it's God who's at fault for forsaking such devoted followers, I mused. The same God had abandoned Asia, so I couldn't help but hate Him myself.

"The main hall is located directly past the entrance. We should storm it together. The hard part will be finding the trapdoor to the basement and dealing with any assassins lying in wait for us."

Assassins… That word alone raised the hairs on the back of my neck.

We exchanged glances in the faint moonlight outside the church and nodded as one. We were ready! All we had to do now was barge in! *Hold on, Asia!* I thought.

Bang!

We dove through the entrance and rushed to the main hall. There was no doubting that the fallen angels would have detected us by now. They would know we'd entered their territory. In other words, there was no going back. We had to push forward! I threw the large double doors open and stepped into the nave.

Inside were an altar and several rows of long pews. It looked the same as any other church. The candles and electric lights along the walls let off a dim, yellow illumination. But there *was* something off about the place. It was the crucifix behind the altar. Someone had snapped its head clean off.

What a creepy setting...

Clap, clap, clap. All of a sudden, a figure emerged from behind a pillar, putting his hands together in exaggerated delight. No sooner did I make out his face than raw disgust welled up inside me.

"Welcome! What a joyous reunion!" It was that white-haired, psycho priest—Freed or whatever his name was! He was the one they'd left lying in wait for us. The guy was wearing that same freaky grin as last time.

"Here's the thing," he began, "I make a point of never meeting the same demons twice. You see, with strength like mine, I pride myself on butchering any one of you I come across *on the spot*! Then I kiss their lifeless corpses good-bye! *That's* my purpose in life! But then you guys *had* to go and ruin my style! No, I will *not* abide you ruining my life's work! You really piss me off! You're going to die today, you hear me?! You maggot demons!" The priest had practically cycled through the full range of human emotion before settling on primal, uncontrollable rage.

The priest reached into his pockets and retrieved his gun and bladeless sword. An electric vibration buzzed through the air as he activated his blade. I couldn't afford to get hit by that or by his gun. This time around, though, it was three against one.

"You *pathetic* demons are here to save Asia, no? Ha-ha! How *kindhearted* of you, coming after that dirty, devil-loving wretch of a sister! She would have been better off ending her own life the second she fell for one of *you*!"

What's that supposed to mean?! "Where is she?!" I demanded.

"Oh, all you have to do is take the stairs beneath the altar to the basement. You'll find them performing the ritual down there." Freed motioned toward the altar with his blade, casually revealing the location of the secret entrance.

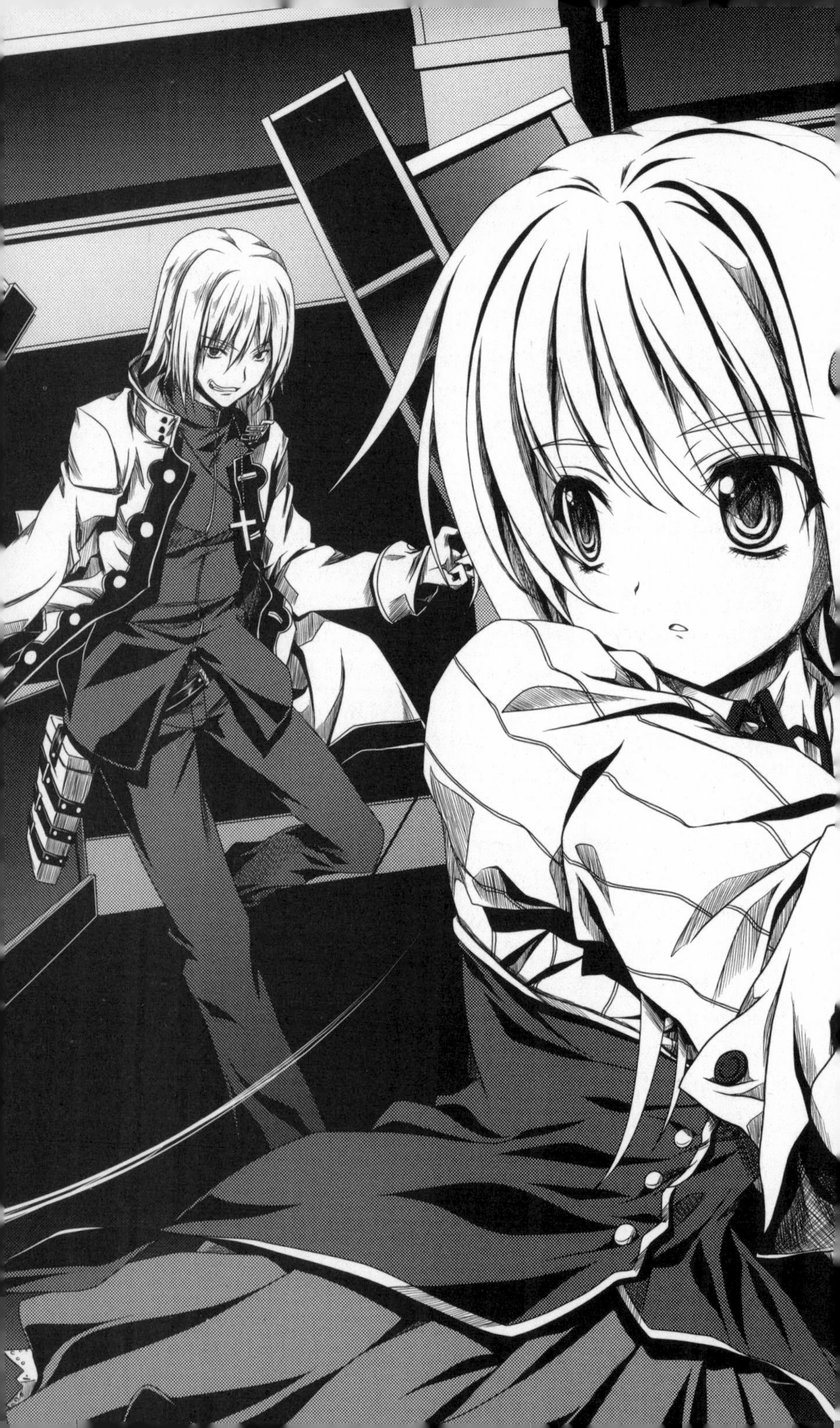

Hold on, isn't he supposed to be stopping us? Or is he so confident he can defeat us all that he doesn't mind revealing where she is?

"Sacred Gear!" I cried, activating the red gauntlet. My Sacred Gear had been successfully equipped! I had this! Kiba drew his sword from its scabbard, just as Koneko— *Whoa!* I was so shocked by what I saw that I thought my eyes would pop out.

Koneko had lifted one of the pews, which was several times longer than she was tall, into the air.

"…Here."

Whoosh! With a powerful lunge, she hurled the bench directly at the priest! No way in hell had he seen that superhuman attack coming!

"Heh! You're pretty strong for a runt!" Freed spun to the side, slicing through the airborne pew with a single stroke of his blade. Both halves fell harmlessly to the ground.

"My turn." No sooner did Kiba enter the corner of my vision than he disappeared. Actually, it would have been better to say he was moving faster than my eyes could keep up!

Clang! Sparks flew as he brought his sword down on the priest's blade. So Freed's weapon *was* solid, even if did look like it was made of pure light. Each time it clashed against Kiba's, a shrill, metallic sound rang out.

"Urgh! Argh! Is that all you've got?! Show me something interesting! Let's save the last words until *after* you're dead!"

Kiba spiraled through the air, dodging the soundless projectiles that flew toward him, always maintaining the pressure of his own attacks. In fact, he evaded each and every one of the priest's shots. I was astounded. Not to be outdone, Freed was avoiding Kiba's assault with equal precision. They went at it again and again.

I might not have been able to catch Kiba's movements, but by the looks of it, the priest could. Yep, I wouldn't have stood a chance against Freed by myself. Kiba and the priest exchanged baleful glares as their swords locked together.

"You're strong, I'll give you that."

"Ha-ha! Impressive! And *you're* a Knight! What perfect movements! Wonderful! I haven't had a good fight in ages! I was starting to feel a little bored! Ha-ha, yes! I'm going to enjoy killing you!"

"All right. If you want to get serious about this, I can, too."

Hold on, that's not them already serious?!

"Eat this." I almost didn't even recognize that intense, almost inaudible voice as Kiba's. The moment he spoke, a black wave poured out of his sword, enveloping it in a deep, writhing fog.

Darkness. That was the only word that sprang to mind. The shadow had completely encased Kiba's weapon—or rather, it had *become* his weapon. When it next collided with the priest's sword of light, it began consuming it.

"Wh-what the hell is this?!" Freed cried out in alarm.

"The Holy Eraser—a weapon that devours light."

"Y-you've got a Sacred Gear, too?!"

A Sacred Gear?! Kiba?! Damn, that blade of darkness looks awesome! Hold on, so the popular pretty boys get all the coolest weapons, too?!

It wasn't long before Kiba's sword completely extinguished Freed's blade, leaving it unable to maintain its form. This was my chance. I charged straight for that psycho.

"Sacred Gear! Activate!"

"Boost!" A powerful voice boomed from the jewel embedded in my gauntlet, and my whole body surged with energy. My attack was aimed at the priest, but he'd seen me coming for him.

"How many times do I have to say it?! You really are *pissing me off*!" He leveled his gun right at me, blasting me with another soundless projectile.

This was it! "Promotion: *Rook*!" I cried out. The bullet ricocheted off me, vanishing.

"Promotion?! You're a Pawn?!" Freed was clearly taken aback.

Yep, I'm a Pawn! And this Pawn is gonna crush you! "A Rook's key attributes are incredible defense—," I began, lifting my fist in front of his face. There was a strange, stiff sensation in my hand, but I didn't let that stop me from letting loose. Freed was sent flying backward across the room. "—and unparalleled strength!"

I broke into a weak chuckle as I caught my breath. "That was for hitting Asia... Heh, it felt pretty good, actually."

Freed hauled himself up from the ground, spitting out a mouthful of blood. His right cheek was badly swollen.

That's it? It seemed promoting myself to a Rook wasn't enough to match Koneko's power.

Hold on... Upon closer inspection, I saw that the hilt of Freed's sword had been completely shattered. *Did he use it to shield himself?* I wondered. That must have been the sensation I'd felt. He was fast, that was for sure.

"...Urgh... Not only do I get smashed by a demon, but now he's mouthing off to me..." Freed let out a shrill howl. "You bastard! Don't get *cocky* with me, you *miserable little demon*! I'll kill you! I'll carve you into a million pieces, you disgusting maggot! *Die!*" he screamed as he pulled a second hilt from his robes.

Another one? How many does he have?! Regardless, Kiba, Koneko, and I had him completely surrounded.

Realizing we had him cornered, the stray priest broke out into a distressed smirk. "Urgh... I'll be damned if a bunch of demons are going to get the best of Freed Sellzen! You may have won the battle, but not the war! I'm going to rue not being able to exorcise you scum, but falling back beats dying!" He pulled a small, round orb from his pocket, slamming it to the ground. Suddenly, an intense, blinding light erupted from it, blinding us for a moment.

A smoke screen?! By the time I could make out my surroundings, Freed had already escaped.

At that moment, however, the psycho's voice called out from the darkness: "Hey, runt! Issei, was it? I think I've fallen in love with you. You didn't think you could get away with hitting me and then mouthing off like that, did you? I'm going to slaughter you, you hear? Just you wait—I'll be back. Until then, suckers!"

I scanned the room, but there was no sign of him. He'd run away and even left with a parting shot. Whatever. I didn't have time to waste thinking about him. I exchanged silent nods with Kiba and Koneko. Together, we headed for the hidden entrance beneath the altar.

—○●○—

The three of us made our way down the winding staircase into the basement. Judging by the lights lining the corridor, the electricity extended down here. Kiba took the lead as we proceeded, first down the staircase and then through a long passageway into the basement.

Several doors lined the corridor, but our destination was straight ahead.

"Through here, I think... I can smell her..." Koneko pointed down the corridor.

So Asia's here? That was enough to boost my spirits. *Hold on, Asia. I'm coming for you!*

At the end of the passageway stood a huge door. "Is this it?" I asked.

"Probably. I think we'll find quite a few exorcists inside. Maybe even a fallen angel. Are you ready?" Kiba turned to the two of us. Koneko and I nodded. "All right. Then let's get this door—"

Just as Kiba and I moved to force it, though, the door began swinging open entirely on its own. A heavy, grating sound rumbled through the corridor as the ritual site gradually came into view.

"Welcome, demons," said Raynare, the fallen angel, from the deepest part of the room. The chamber was filled with priests, each grasping the hilt of a sword of light.

"Asia!" I cried out after laying eyes on the figure chained to the cross near Raynare.

She lifted her head. "...Issei?"

"We're here to save you!" I said with a warm smile.

"Issei..." Tears began dripping down Asia's cheeks.

"What a touching reunion, but I'm afraid you're too late. The ritual is almost over."

Almost over? What does that—?

All of a sudden, Asia's body began glowing. "…Argh, ahhhhhhh-hhh!" Her pained screams filled the room.

"Asia!" I moved to reach her, but before I could get anywhere, I found myself surrounded by priests.

"No you don't!"

"Demons! We'll destroy you!"

"Get out of my way, you damned priests! I don't have time to deal with you all!"

Bang! There was a loud thump as Koneko punched one of the acolytes away. "…Don't touch me," she murmured.

Kiba had drawn his blade. "Looks like I'm going to have to go all in. I really hate priests, you know. Allow me to devour that light of yours." There was a sharp glint to his eyes, keen enough to send shivers down my spine. His sword of darkness was clearly thirsty for blood. This was no doubt going to be an all-out war.

"Noooooooo…!" A large radiance emerged from Asia's body and floated slowly into Raynare's hand.

"At last! How long I've been lusting after this power! The Sacred Gear! Those miserable hearts are in the palm of my hand!" Raynare embraced that light, her face twisting in ecstasy. It grew more brilliant, illuminating the entire room. Soon after, it died down, shrouding the fallen angel in a bright-green glow.

"Hee-hee-hee, ha-ha-ha-ha-ha-ha-ha! Absolute power! With this, I will be the strongest fallen angel there is! All those fools who screwed me over will rue the day they decided to cross *me*!" Raynare cackled with laughter.

I paid her no heed as I charged straight for Asia. The priests moved to block my path, but Kiba and Koneko lashed out to knock them out of my way. Kiba's sword consumed the priests' blades of light while

Koneko moved to crush her now-defenseless foes. The two fought together in flawless unison, complementing each other's strengths and weaknesses with a precision that belied their long experience and training.

"Thanks, both of you!" I finally made my way to Asia, who was bound to the crucifix.

She's okay, right? She has to be! I untied her arms and legs and embraced her limp body.

"...I-Issei..."

"Asia, I came back for you."

"...Thank you..." Her voice was small and weak, almost sapped of life.

Hey, hang in there! She's gonna be okay, right? Come on, don't tell me...

"It's too late." Raynare broke into a cold sneer as she saw the worry in my eyes. "Now that her Sacred Gear has been torn from her, she will die."

"Then give it back!" I howled, but her cruel grin only widened.

"I don't think so. Do you realize I had to fool my own superiors to get my hands on this? Now all that's left to do is destroy the evidence—starting with you."

"Damn you... You're nothing like the Yuuma I remember."

At this, Raynare broke into a shrill laugh. "Ah-ha-ha-ha! It was fun dating you."

"...You were my first girlfriend..."

"Heh, and *you* were so wet behind the ears. I must admit, there's nothing quite like an inexperienced boy like yourself."

"...I was serious about you."

"Heh-heh-heh, and you treated me well. Whenever I found myself in a spot of trouble, you were there to set things right. But you realize I orchestrated it all, don't you? You can be pretty amusing when you get worked up."

"...I put my heart and soul into our first date. I wanted to make it a wonderful memory for both of us."

"Ah-ha-ha-ha! Oh? But it was so *ordinary*! You can't imagine how bored I was!"

"...Yuuma."

"Heh-heh-heh... Do you know why I chose that name? *Yuuma*—it's written with the characters for *evening* and *hemp*. Because I intended from the very beginning to kill you at dusk. Beautiful, don't you think, Issei?"

By now, my rage had bubbled over. "Raynaaaaare!"

"Ah-ha-ha-ha! A spoiled brat like you has no right to utter my true name," she sneered.

My insides were positively seething with hatred. I had never encountered a more despicable person in my life. *She* was the real demon here!

"Hyoudou!" Kiba called out. "We can't defend ourselves here! Let's retreat back upstairs! Koneko and I will open a path for you! Quickly!" He began mowing down the nearest group of acolytes.

He was right. There were still a lot of priests remaining, and on top of that, I wouldn't be able to protect Asia and fight the fallen angel at the same time. I fixed Raynare with a baleful glare, took Asia in my arms, and dashed for the entrance.

"Koneko, let's clear a path for Hyoudou!" Kiba cried.

"...Understood."

The two of them worked to take out the seemingly endless stream of lackeys who tried to bar my way. With their help, I managed to make it back to the entrance corridor.

"Kiba! Koneko!"

"Go on ahead! We'll keep them occupied here!"

"...Go."

"But—"

"Get a move on!"

Dammit, Kiba, Koneko! Quit showing off! I had no choice but to rely on them. They were my superiors when it came to demon life, after all. I trusted they weren't foolish enough to let themselves get killed!

"Kiba! Koneko! When this is all over, I want you to call me Issei! We're friends!" I felt as if I could sense them both smiling behind me. With that, I hurried back through the tunnel that led to the surface.

Grasping Asia tightly in my arms, I emerged from the hidden staircase back into the hall.

There was definitely something wrong with her. Asia's face was deathly pale. I laid her down on a nearby bench. "Hold on, Asia! Once we get out of here, you're free! Stay with me! We've still got so much to look forward to!"

She flashed me a weak smile and took my hand. There was no strength, no warmth left in her grip. "...I know it wasn't a very long time...but I'm so blessed...to have made a friend like you..." She widened her lips in a pained smile. "...If I'm ever reborn...please be my friend...again..."

"Wh-what are you saying?! It isn't over, okay?! I'm gonna take you to all kinds of fun places! Karaoke! Arcades! Bowling! And so many others, too! Hang in there!" Tears traced their way down my face. I was trying so hard to keep her smiling, but I couldn't even stop myself from crying. I knew what was happening. Asia was dying. Try as I might, there was no denying that.

This can't be happening. It can't be.

"We're friends! Always! That's right! I still need to introduce you to Matsuda and Motohama! They might come across as pervs, but they're actually pretty nice guys! I'm sure they'd love to be your friends, too! We'll have so much fun together, you won't even believe it!"

"...I wish...I'd been born in this country... Then I could have gone to school with you...Issei..."

"You can! As soon as you want!"

Asia brushed her hand weakly against my cheek. "…You're crying… for me… Now…I don't have any more…" Her hand fell slowly to her side. "…Thank you…"

Those were her final words to me. With a joyful smile, Asia's spirit left her. I felt my strength wane. All I could do was sit there, staring into her motionless face. My tears wouldn't stop flowing.

Why?! Why did she have to die like this?! She was a good person! A kind, gentle person who wanted nothing more than to heal those in need! Why wouldn't anyone be her friend? Why did it take me until now to reach her side?!

"God?! I know you're there!" I shouted at the top of my lungs to the ceiling of the church. "If demons and angels exist, then you must, too! You're watching this, aren't you?! You've been watching the whole damn time, haven't you?!" I didn't know who I expected to answer, but I still wailed my lungs out. "Don't take her away! Please! Bring her back! I beg you! She hasn't done anything wrong! All she wanted was to make friends! I'll be here for her forever! So please! Let her smile again! Please, God!" Despite my pleas, there was no response.

"Is this my fault?! Did you abandon her because of me?! Because I'm a demon?" I ground my teeth in frustration. I'd been unable to do anything. I was powerless.

If I'd been stronger, if I'd possessed more skill and ability as a demon… If I'd just been able to save her… No matter how much I regretted it, though, I thought for sure I'd never see Asia's beautiful smile again.

"Well, well, a demon asking God for forgiveness? Or was it a wish?" Raynare's voice taunted me from behind. I spun around, only to see the fallen angel grinning scornfully at me.

"Would you look at this? That Knight managed to injure me on my way up here," she said, placing a hand atop her wound. A pale-green light flowed forth, sealing the deep gash.

"Wonderful, isn't it? No matter the injury, I heal instantly. A perfect gift for those of us who no longer have the benefit of divine protection, wouldn't you say?"

Damn you. That light belonged to Asia. What gave her the right to use it? And what had happened to Kiba and Koneko? Were they okay?

"A fallen angel with the power to heal other fallen angels. Now I'll never lose my rank in the underworld. Almighty Azazel and Shemhazai, I am prepared and ready to do your work! There's nothing more wonderful than this! Ah, Azazel… I dedicate my power, this power, to you!"

"What does that matter?" I demanded, glaring viciously. "What does any of it matter? Fallen angels, God, demons… What did any of them have to do with Asia?!"

"Oh, but they had everything to do with her. She was specifically chosen as the bearer of this Sacred Gear."

"…You could still have let her live a quiet life. A normal life."

"I'm afraid not. Those who possess exceptional Sacred Gears are always ostracized by society. Their powers simply set them apart. Come now, you know how much humans hate those who are different, no matter how wonderful that difference might make them."

"…I—I would have protected her! As her friend!"

"Ah-ha-ha-ha! Impossible! She's dead, isn't she? Stone-cold dead! You couldn't save her that evening, and you can't save her now! You're a funny one! *Very* amusing!"

"…I know I failed her. I'll never forgive you…or myself." I was the one who had been unable to save her, even if it was Raynare who dealt the killing blow.

All of a sudden, Rias's words from earlier flashed through my mind—

"—Just feel. Sacred Gears are driven by your feelings. That goes for their overall power as well."

"Give her back."

"—Emotions are precious, even to demons. The stronger they are, the more powerful your Sacred Gear will become."

*   *   *

"Give her back to me!"

"Dragon Booster!" The Sacred Gear enveloping my arm activated in response to my cry, the jewel in the center of the gauntlet radiating a dazzling light. A strange symbol appeared on the back of the it. At the same time, a rush of energy surged through me, flowing from the Sacred Gear into my own body.

Reinvigorated, I dashed forward and swung my fist at my smirking opponent.

Raynare dodged my strikes effortlessly, as if executing an intricate dance.

"Let me put this in a way even an idiot like you can understand: Our respective power levels are simply too different. If I'm at level one thousand, you're stuck at level one. You can't hope to match me. Even using that Sacred Gear of yours, doubling your power still only raises you to level two. It's futile! You can't possibly beat me! Ah-ha-ha-ha!"

"Boost!" The jewel in the back of the gauntlet sounded once more, the symbol glowing inside the jewel changing from *I* to *II*.

Thud! Something else had changed, deep inside my body. The power within me—the strength to defeat the enemy before me was multiplying rapidly.

"Rrraaaaah!" I charged after Raynare, concentrating that energy into my fist. The fact that I had been promoted into a Rook earlier likely made a difference, too.

"Heh! Gathering your strength? It isn't enough!" The fallen angel dodged my attacks again. In an instant, Raynare gathered a ball of light in each hand, stretching the orbs into familiar shapes. "Let's see how you handle these!"

Ngh! The spears of light tore through both my legs, cutting deep into my thighs. Even with the increased defenses of a Rook, I hadn't been able to withstand them.

"Gwaaaaaaaaaargh!" I howled in agony as pain coursed through my body, but with both spears still embedded in my legs, I couldn't even fall to my knees. I grabbed them with my bare hands and pulled.

"Gwaaaaaaaaaargh!" I could smell my flesh searing. Damn, those things were hot! It must've been because they were made of light. My palms were already scorched black. Smoke rose from my hands and the wounds in my legs. The pain was unbearable.

Raynare broke into a mocking laugh as she watched me attempt to remove the spears. "Ah-ha-ha-ha! Just how stupid are you? Light is poison to demons. Merely touching it is enough to scorch your flesh. For your kind, there is no greater torment! For a low-level demon like you—"

"Grrraaaaah!" With a raw, primal howl, I squeezed the spears tighter and yanked them, inch by inch, out of my flesh. My legs were screaming in agony. The intense pain tore through me mercilessly. I felt as if I would pass out, like I would fall dead if I didn't grit my teeth hard enough, but I kept going.

"This... This is nothing compared to what you put Asia through!" Tears and sweat dripping down my face, I continued wrenching out the spears. My legs were howling in pain. Still, I knew I could do it! I had to!

Splosh. With a sickening noise and a splash of blood, I'd finally managed to free myself.

The second I released my grip on those projectiles, they dissipated into thin air before even hitting the ground. No longer stanched by the spears, my blood began pooling rapidly at my feet. Removing the fallen angel's weapons, though, hadn't stopped the searing ache.

"Boost!" My last attack may have failed, but even so, the gauntlet on my hand let out a deep, bellowing roar. Despite my increased power, the pain was torturous. Tears continued washing down my face, and drool dripped from my chin.

Wha—?! My strength abandoned me, and I slipped hard onto the floor. I wasn't even able to muster the energy to pull myself up.

Dammit! My legs, my whole body, had been completely sapped of power. To say I was in a bad spot was putting it lightly.

"...You know, I really am impressed. A lower-class demon rooting out not one but two spears of light? But you're fighting the inevitable. My light might not be particularly flashy, but at that density, it's incredibly efficient at killing demons. So efficient, in fact, that I gifted it to my priests to use in their own weapons. Even a middle-class demon would have difficulty recovering from a single strike. As for one of your rank? Heh-heh-heh, don't underestimate the power of light. Especially *mine*." Raynare sure seemed to enjoy the sound of her own voice.

"It's already circulating throughout your body, whittling away at you piece by piece. If you don't get healed soon, that will be it. Heh. Frankly, I expected you'd have already kicked the bucket by now. You're stronger than you look."

Ah... So for a newbie demon like me, these are mortal wounds... I had guessed as much. My whole body was screaming in an agony that went beyond normal pain. It felt like my bones, my flesh, everything inside me was being scorched to cinders. And of course, my nerves were on fire, too, so much so that I thought I would go mad. Yep, if I couldn't fix this soon, I was done for. And yet...

There was no way I was just gonna sit here, but my legs refused to move. Was this the end? I glanced toward Asia. She looked like she was sleeping quietly.

Sorry for making such a ruckus, I thought to her. *I'll be okay. I'm stronger than I look. Really, I'll be fine. See?* At the very least, I didn't want Asia worrying about me.

"I guess it's times like this that people turn to God for salvation..." The words slipped from my mouth without my even realizing.

"...?" Raynare raised an eyebrow in bewilderment, but I kept talking.

"But He isn't gonna help me. He didn't answer me before, and He never lifted a finger to help Asia. Ha. Some deity He is."

"What are you going on about? Don't tell me you've finally lost it?"

"What was I thinking? It's Satan I should be praying to. You're listening, aren't you? I'm a demon now, so what do you say? I need a little help."

"...You really have lost your mind. Blabbering to yourself won't do you any good."

"Give me the strength to pulverize this fallen angel! I don't need you to strike her down for me. I don't need backup. I can do it. Me. See, I can stand up by myself. Just give me one good go. My rage is burning so strong, I can take the pain. One hit will be enough... Just let me crush her!"

Guh... My legs began moving. I had already lost all sensation in them, and the slightest twitch sent a surge of agony coursing through my body. Still, I could move. I lifted myself up from the floor. My whole body wouldn't stop trembling—but still, I rose to my feet. Though it was unbearable, I could move. I did move. All I needed was enough strength to deal one blow.

"—! I-impossible! How are you able to stand?! That light should be—" Raynare froze in utter shock as I slowly forced my way toward her.

Then, with my feet quaking and blood still gushing from my wounds, I stood directly in front of her. "Hey, ex-girlfriend. I guess I should thank you."

"...I don't believe it! A low-class demon shouldn't even be able to stand with your injuries! That light must be burning you from the inside out! You shouldn't have the ability to temper it!"

"Don't get me wrong; it's not like it just tickles or anything. I feel like I'm about to pass out. But I don't care! My hatred for you will overcome anything!" I fixed Raynare with an unwavering, unyielding glare. I was sure my next move would be my last. I wouldn't be able to hold out any longer than that. I had to finish this in one strike. I had to make it count.

"What do you say, Sacred Gear? We've still got enough strength left to send this fallen angel flying, huh? Let's finish this."

"Explosion!" The powerful voice blasted out with immense energy. The jewel embedded in the gauntlet released a blinding light. Unlike the light wielded by the fallen angel, however, this filled me not with unbearable pain but a sense of peace. It reminded me of the pale-green glow of Asia's healing technique. I could feel my strength welling up inside me.

So there are some kinds of light demons thrive on. I stepped forward. Blood spurted from the wounds in my legs. I could taste it in the back of my throat, too. I was in a bad way, that was for sure. There was no limit to the sheer agony I was experiencing. My head rang in torment, but it was fine. I could still move.

Even in this sorry state, raw power flowed from the gauntlet into my body. When I had encountered Raynare earlier this evening, the chasm between our levels had been terrifying. My instincts had all but cowered at her overwhelming presence, and my body had completely frozen. I'd been sure I didn't stand a chance.

Not so now.

The energy flowing out of my gauntlet was incredible. Nonetheless, as the bearer of this Sacred Gear, I knew it wouldn't last forever. This boost was a one-time use only. The second I unleashed it on my foe, it would be gone forever. My Sacred Gear told me as much. Not verbally, of course, but physically.

I readied myself to unleash my final punch. I didn't have any fighting experience, but that was fine. All it would take was one hit. My target was this godforsaken fallen angel in front of me. I wasn't about to miss.

"…Impossible. Wh-what are you doing…?! Your Sacred Gear shouldn't be anywhere near that strong…! It…it's just a Twice Critical…! It can't be. H-how could you possibly surpass me…? That energy wave is at least middle-class…no, high-class…?!"

This power's equal to a high-class demon's? Is this the Sacred Gear's doing?

Hey, come on, I thought you were just supposed to double my power?

The only high-class demon I'd ever met was Rias. Did that mean I was about as strong as her now?

"Impossible! I have the supreme healing power! Now that I hold the Twilight Healing, I've reached the ultimate level! I've earned the love of Azazel and Shemhazai! I—I can't lose to a lowly demon like you!" Raynare summoned fresh spears of light in both hands, hurling them with all her might.

I brushed the projectiles aside with my fist, and both dissipated into thin air.

Watching me deflect her frenzied attack with such ease, Raynare grew pale. "N-no!"

Flap! Her black wings beat back and forth loudly as she prepared to leap into the air.

After all that high-and-mighty talk, she's trying to escape now? Is she the kind to hightail it the second the tide turns against her? No matter what type she was, I wasn't about to let Raynare get away. No way in hell!

I leaped after her the second she left the ground, grabbing her arm. I couldn't believe how fast I'd moved. It had been so quick that even Raynare hadn't been able to react in time.

Her arm was thin and meager. I pulled her toward me, refusing to let go. "You won't get away!"

"No! I have the supreme power!"

"Go to hell, you goddamned angel!"

"You lowly demon!"

"Hraaaaah!" In one fell burst, I unleashed the energy that had built up in the gauntlet, concentrating my whole being on that one, final punch. I directed the blow straight into the face of my hated enemy.

Crack! There was a cruel breaking sound as my fist caved in Raynare's skull then just kept going even harder. The force of the impact sent her flying backward across the room.

Crash! The fallen angel smashed into the far wall, tearing a gaping hole in the stone edifice and sending dust billowing through the air. When the cloud finally settled, I saw her lying sprawled on the ground outside. Raynare wasn't moving. I couldn't tell whether she was dead or not, but whatever the case, she clearly wasn't about to get back up.

"Serves you right." I curled my lips in a faint grin. Really, that had felt good.

But it wasn't long before my exultation turned to anguish.

"…Asia."

I would never see her smile again.

Having used up every ounce of my energy defeating the fallen angel, I slumped weakly to the floor. Suddenly, someone grabbed my shoulder. It was Kiba.

"Look at you, taking down a fallen angel on your own," he said as he helped me stay on my feet. To my surprise, he didn't look in particularly good shape himself.

"What held you up?"

Kiba let out a chuckle. "I was instructed to stay back."

Rias?

"That's right. I trusted you to defeat Raynare by yourself." I turned toward the new voice only to find Rias approaching me with a gentle smile and a flourish of her crimson hair.

"Prez? Where did you come from?"

"The basement. Once my business was finished, I used the magic circle to jump down there. I've never teleported into a church before. I admit I was a little worried," she said with a sigh.

So that's how she showed up at the same time as Kiba and Koneko. That must have meant they'd defeated the priests. Those guys wouldn't have stood much of a chance against Rias.

At that moment, Koneko walked briskly past me. *Where's she going?* I wondered.

Rias drew closer and planted herself directly in front of me. "I'm glad to see that you won."

"P-Prez... Ha, I guess I did, didn't I?"

"Wonderful. I expected no less of a member of my Familia." She let out a chuckle before wrinkling her nose.

"Oh dear, this place is a mess. President, are you all right?" Akeno looked troubled.

"...Is something wrong?" I asked nervously.

"Churches are the domain of God—or rather, of religions dedicated to Him—even if they are being used by fallen angels. Normally, if demons like us were to lay a church to waste like this, we would risk finding ourselves targeted for assassination."

S-seriously?!

"We should be okay this time, though."

"...Why's that?"

"This building had been abandoned for quite some time. A band of fallen angels and their followers might have made use of it, and we may have picked a fight with them, but we didn't officially cross into their territory. *That* might have started a war. This was just a small scuffle between a single demon and a lone fallen angel, though. These things happen all the time. We should be okay."

Right... I guess you could frame it that way, I thought, relieved.

"President, I brought her." Koneko appeared once more through the hole that had been blasted through the wall, dragging a heavy load behind her.

She was hauling the unconscious Raynare back inside by one of her misshapen black wings. *Hold on, "brought"...? That's an interesting way to put it.*

"Thank you, Koneko. Now then, what say we wake her up. Akeno?"

"Very good." Akeno raised her hand, and a pale ball of something that looked like water floated up before her.

Another one of her demon powers? I guessed.

Akeno dropped the airborne mass directly atop the fallen angel, dousing her in water.

There was a loud splash, followed by a gurgling cough. Raynare slowly opened her eyes only to find Rias staring down from above her.

"Nice to meet you, fallen angel Raynare."

"...The Gremory girl...?"

"Greetings. I am Rias Gremory, the next head of the House of Gremory," the prez said with a composed smile. "It's wonderful to meet you. Such a shame we don't have long to chat."

Raynare glared up at her before breaking out into a sneer. "...You think you've beaten me, but you're mistaken. We might have kept our plan from the higher-ups, but there are other fallen angels working with me. Once they realize I'm in danger, they'll—"

"I'm afraid they won't be coming." Rias cut her off. "I've already disposed of the fallen angels Kalavana, Dohnaseek, and Mittelt."

"You're lying!" Raynare balked, sitting up straight.

Rias pulled three large black feathers from her pocket. "These belonged to them. They were your brethren, so you can tell them apart, I presume?"

At this sight, Raynare's expression darkened. It looked like Rias was telling the truth.

"I guessed there were several fallen angels plotting away in this town back when Dohnaseek first attacked Issei. I assumed at the time that they were working on something collectively and so chose to ignore it. Even I'm not foolish enough to take you all on. But then I heard how your associates were lurking in the shadows, trying to keep a low profile, so I brought Akeno with me thinking to talk to them. And what would you know? They spilled your whole plan without me even needing to ask. By helping you, they hoped to elevate their own status in your society. Lowlifes like that have an unfortunate habit of boasting about how clever they think they are." Rias twisted her lips scornfully. Raynare could only grit her teeth in frustration.

"Two young ladies approaching them alone? They must have underestimated us. They told us everything, thinking they'd kill us anyway." Rias chuckled. "How foolish. They were the ones who met their demise. You sure had some pretty pathetic conspirators working on your little scheme."

So that's what it was. That's what Rias had meant by "urgent business." Exterminating the other fallen angels… She'd wanted to help me from the very beginning…even though I'd been so rude to her… I cursed myself. Why did I have to let my emotions get the better of me all the time?

"She can take down any foe with a single shot. The Duke's beloved daughter is truly gifted in the art of destruction. Despite her youth, the president is renowned as a genius in demon society," Kiba whispered to me, extolling Rias's praises.

"Some even call her the Crimson-Haired Princess of Annihilation," Akeno added with a light chuckle.

P-Princess of Annihilation…? What a terrifying nickname…and I'm part of her Familia… I didn't know what to think anymore…

Rias glanced at my left arm—at the gauntlet still equipped to it.

"…The Red Dragon. That mark wasn't there before… I see…" Maybe I was imagining things, but Rias looked almost taken aback.

"That explains how Issei was able to defeat a fallen angel," she murmured quietly. "Do you see that, Raynare? You weren't defeated by a Twice Critical after all. Issei Hyoudou's Sacred Gear is far more special than that."

The fallen angel skeptically raised an eyebrow.

"The Boosted Gear, the Gauntlet of the Red Dragon Emperor—the rarest of the rare," Rias continued. "That emblem of the Red Dragon is proof. I'm sure even you must know what that means."

Hearing this explanation, Raynare's mouth fell open in shock. "Th-the Boosted Gear… One of the sacred, god-destroying Longinuses… It's said to be capable of bestowing power surpassing even that of Satan or God... Are you telling me this *boy* wields such a dev-astating weapon?!"

Rias turned back to me. "If the legends are true, then this Boosted Gear doubles the power of the one wielding it every ten seconds. Even if you begin at level one, you can surpass even the highest-ranked demons and fallen angels with enough time. Who knows—if you can master it, you might even be able to vanquish God Himself."

Seriously, Rias? I can even take down God?! That's this Sacred Gear's hidden power? Indeed, there was an emblem depicting a red dragon carved into the back of the gauntlet. That must have been why it kept sounding *Boost!* every so often. Each time it did, it must have been doubling my power. It certainly explained why I kept growing stronger. Could it have also been the reason Raynare had suddenly become so terrified of me toward the end of our fight?

What a formidable Sacred Gear... I returned my gaze to the weapon encompassing my left arm with a renewed nervousness. The Boosted Gear. My Sacred Gear. I still couldn't believe it... *Does this mean I've been promised some kind of legendary rise through the ranks of demonkind?!*

"Well, as powerful as it is, a Sacred Gear that requires so much time to charge comes with considerable risk. Few opponents would sit by and wait for it to reach its full potential. Luckily for you, Raynare here got more than a little carried away."

Ugh. Rias had hit the nail on the head there. She was right, of course. It seemed foolish to think an opponent would just wait around and let me power up. In other words, my Sacred Gear was immensely power-ful but also came with a notable weakness.

Rias stepped toward me. A sweet, intoxicating scent wafted from her crimson hair.

She gently patted my head as she spoke. "Most interesting. I'm so pleased to have you as my manservant, Issei. I might not be able to contain my affection for you." With that, she let out a light chuckle.

Though she regarded me kindly, I found myself trembling with a terror of an altogether different sort.

"P-Prez..."

"What is it?" she asked, her smile unwavering.

Struck by a sense of shame, I bowed my head to her. "I'm sorry. I said some pretty awful stuff earlier... I thought you weren't going to help Asia, but I was wrong... I had no idea you were doing so much..." I owed her my deepest apologies. I'd assumed she truly was a cold-hearted demon, so I'd thrown insult after insult at her. Now that it was all over, all I could do was apologize.

Surprisingly, Rias didn't seem bothered. She continued patting my head. Before I knew it, tears began pouring down my cheeks. I hadn't been able to accomplish my goal.

"P-Prez... I—I couldn't...save Asia..."

"There's no need to cry. No one can blame you for what happened."

"But... But I..."

She wiped away my tears with her fingertip. "Don't blame yourself. You're still getting used to being a demon. There is still much for you to learn; that's all there is to it. Improve yourself. Become stronger. I'm going to work you hard from now, so be ready, Issei the Pawn."

"Okay..."

I have to try my hardest. I'm gonna get stronger no matter what! I etched those words into my heart.

"Now then, it's time I finished my work." With that, Rias's eyes turned frigid and ruthless. She approached Raynare. The fallen angel was clearly terrified.

"Begone." Rias's tone was colder than cold, overflowing with murderous intent. "Of course, I will be taking that Sacred Gear back from you as well."

"Y-you've got to be kidding me! Th-this healing power is for Azazel and Shemhazai—"

"It's a wonderful thing, living one's life for the sake of love, but I'm afraid you're a rather tainted individual who lacks a sense of elegance. I can't forgive that." Rias fixed Raynare in her gaze.

There was no question Rias meant to annihilate Raynare.

"Mind if I drop in?" At that moment, a figure appeared in the gaping hole in the wall. It was the priest—Freed Sellzen.

That lunatic! What's he doing back here after turning tail like that?!

"Whoa! Looks like my boss is in a pinch! Whatever shall I do?"

"Help me!" Raynare cried out to him. "Name your reward—it's yours!"

Freed broke out into a lecherous sneer. "Hmm. Hmm. An order from my *esteemed* angel? Can I sleep with you, then? I've always wanted to bed an angel. What higher honor could there be? What better way to elevate my status?"

"Urgh… Q-quit screwing around and help me!" Raynare's face contorted in anger. She looked frantic to make her escape.

Raynare was definitely getting impatient. If I could've read her mind, I'd have bet she was undoubtedly thinking *This measly human will never betray me!*

"Oh, no, no, no, no, no, no, no. I'm serious… This one simple request shouldn't be too much, should it now, my dear angel? Is it? Oh, I see. Well, in that case, I'll bid you adieu. After all, it would be a hell of a gamble. No matter how you look at it, the odds aren't in my favor." Freed spun from side to side, clearly enjoying himself.

"Y-you're a priest, aren't you?! Then save me! You live to serve *me*, you—"

"I refuse to work for a boss who would let herself be beaten by a lowly *demon*. As pleasing as you are to the eye, there isn't much by way of brains in that lofty head of yours. At best, you make good fodder for my carnal fantasies, so you might as well kick the bucket already. Although, as a fallen angel forsaken by God, you won't be finding your way into either Heaven or Hell. Oblivion awaits! Pure nothingness! Ah, there won't be anything left of you. There's nothing but the Three

Jewels of Refuge! Eh, hold on… That's Buddhism! And here I'm supposed to be a Christian! Silly me!" With that, Freed seemed to lose all interest in Raynare.

The fallen angel's face filled with despair. I almost felt sorry for her. Raynare was a mere shadow of the power-hungry and destructive figure she had cut a short time ago.

Freed fixed me with a wide grin. *Huh? Why me?* I thought, displeased.

"Issei, Issei, Issei. What a *wonderful* ability you have there! You've certainly caught my eye! You'll make a worthy kill, that's for sure! Congrats, you've made my top five list of demons to exterminate! Next time we meet, what do you say we have ourselves a romantic, passion-filled fight to the death?"

A cold chill ran down my spine. That psycho priest might have been grinning, but his attitude reeked with the hunger for death. He'd just issued me a challenge—no, advance notice of my own murder.

"Well then, everyone, bye-bye! Don't forget to brush your teeth!" With a casual wave of his hand, he disappeared just as quickly as he'd arrived. Something told me I would be seeing him again. It wasn't a premonition exactly but something more unnerving.

"It looks like your own servant has abandoned you, fallen angel Raynare. You poor thing." Despite her words, there wasn't a hint of sympathy to Rias's voice, and the fallen angel began visibly quivering in trepidation.

Maybe it was because I had once known her only as Yuuma, but I couldn't help feeling somewhat sorry for her. Even if her whole charade as my girlfriend had simply been a plot to lure me into her trap. Raynare stared up at me, her eyes suddenly glistening with love and affection.

"Issei! Help me!" It was Yuuma's voice. "The demon is going to kill me! I love you! I love you, Issei! Please help me defeat her!" Raynare was once again playing the role of my former girlfriend, tearfully begging me to save her life.

I was a fool for feeling sorry for you, Yuuma. "Good-bye, my love… Prez, I can't be the one to do this…" Hearing my final words to her, the fallen angel's expression froze in abject horror.

"…You've toyed with my servant's emotions for the last time. Get out of my sight."

Boom! Rias unleashed a burst of demonic power from the palm of her hand, completely obliterating the fallen angel. All that remained were my vague, lingering emotions and a stray black feather gliding through the air.

—○●○—

A pale-green light filled the church. It was Asia's Sacred Gear. Raynare's defeat seemed to have released it. It bathed me in its warm, comforting glow as Rias took it into her hand.

"Now then, let's say we return this to its rightful owner."

"B-but she's already…" She was already dead. I had failed her. I had sworn to protect her! I had sworn to *save* her! I may have defeated Raynare, but what had been the point of all this if I couldn't even save Asia?

No, I thought. *That kind of attitude is a betrayal to my friends.* They had fought alongside me, for my sake and Asia's. They'd had no personal stake in this.

"…Prez, everyone, I'm really grateful for everything you've all done. B-but Asia…"

"Issei, do you know what this is?" Rias asked as she pulled a small *something* from her pocket.

The item was small and the color of bloodlike crimson, almost the same shade as her hair. A chess piece.

"Huh?"

"This is a Bishop piece, Issei."

"…What?" I was so taken aback by her answer that I didn't know what else to say.

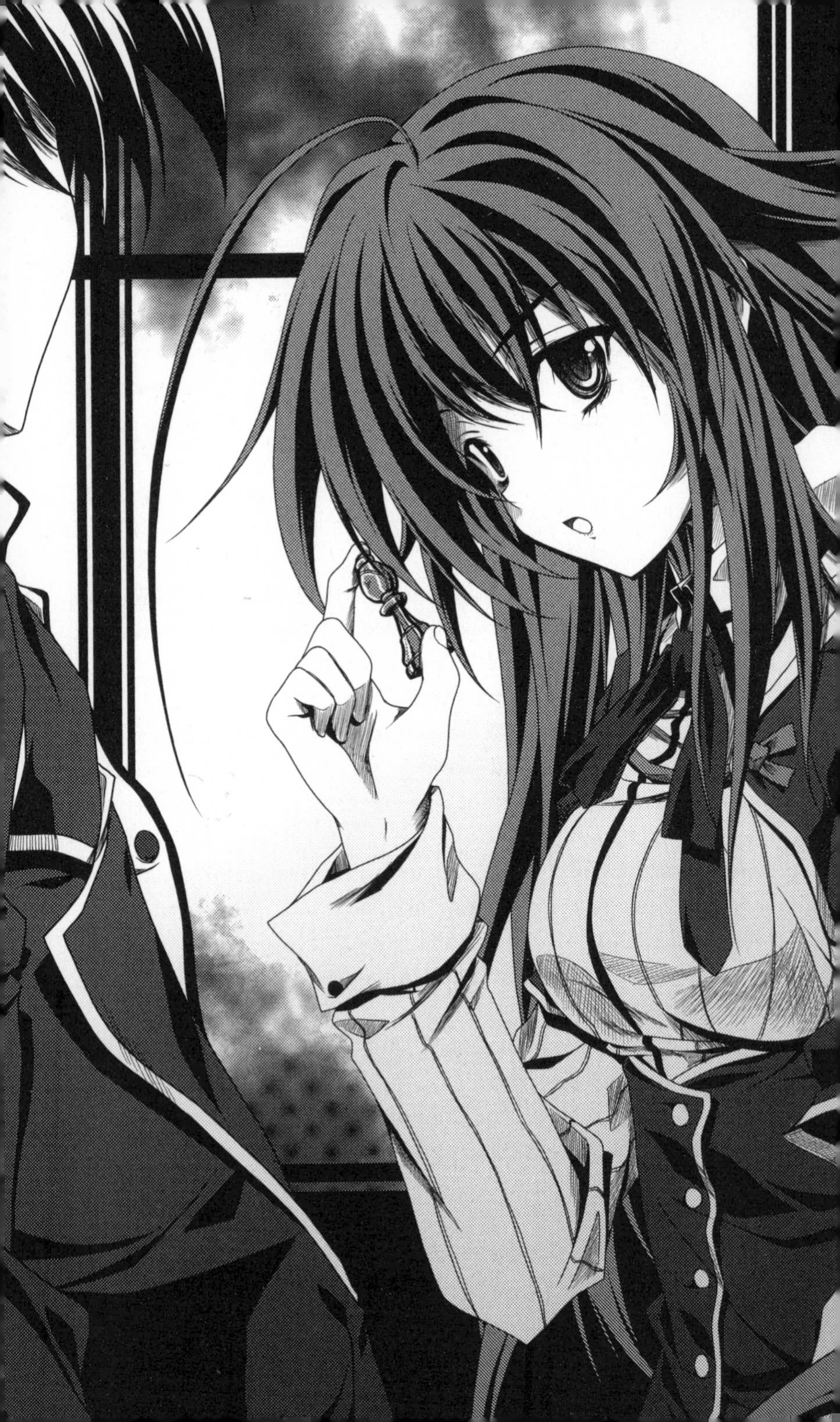

"I neglected to mention this earlier, but noble demons are awarded fifteen Evil Pieces in total: eight Pawns, two Knights, two Bishops, two Rooks, and one Queen. The same one finds in a real game of chess. I've already used one of my Bishops, but I have one remaining."

Rias approached Asia. The nun looked so peaceful in death that it seemed as if she were only sleeping. Rias placed the crimson Bishop piece on Asia's chest.

"The Bishop's role is to protect and support the other demons in the Familia. This girl's healing ability would certainly prove useful. This may be unprecedented, but our good sister is about to be born again into the underworld." A dark, crimson energy began emanating around Rias's body. "I, Rias Gremory, call to thee, Asia Argento! Heed my command! Return thy soul from the shadows of death and rise once more as my demon servant. Rejoice, for thou hast been given life anew as my Bishop!"

The chess piece let out a brilliant, deep-red glow, before sinking into Asia's chest. At the same time, Asia's Sacred Gear let out a pale-green burst of light and sank back inside her as well. Rias watched for a long moment before letting her tremendous energy subside and breathing a deep sigh.

I watched in a trance as Asia began opening her eyes. I could hardly contain my swelling emotions.

"Huh?" It was Asia's voice. I'd thought I'd never hear it again.

Rias flashed me a kind smile. "I won't make a habit of this, but I've resurrected her. Her power to heal our kind may be handy. From now on, Issei, it will be your job to protect her. After all, you *are* her senior now."

Asia sat upright. She glanced around the room for a second until her gaze settled on me. "...Issei?" She cocked her head in bewilderment.

I embraced her with a warm hug. "Let's go home, Asia."

New Life

"Wake up! Get your ass out of bed!"

...I pulled myself to my feet to the sound of an energetic and boyish young woman. I'd set my alarm an hour earlier than usual. Regardless of how sleepy I was, I had business at the clubroom to attend to! No sooner had I put my uniform on than I sped out of the room.

"Ah, you made it." Only Rias was waiting for me when I entered the clubroom.

The school day had yet to start. The previous night, Rias had instructed me to come early to attend a club meeting. She was sitting on one of the sofas, elegantly sipping a cup of tea.

"Morning, Prez."

"Yes, good morning. I take it you're getting used to our early starts?"

"Yep, thanks to you all."

Rias glanced at my legs. "How are your injuries?"

Both of my legs had been badly wounded during the fight the other day, having been impaled yet again by spears of light.

"Thanks to Asia, it's like it never happened," I answered with a grin.

"Oh? Her healing power is proving its worth, then? I can see why the fallen angel wanted it so badly, even going so far as to work behind the backs of her superiors."

I sat on the sofa across from Rias. Since all the excitement at the church, I'd had several burning questions I'd wanted to ask her.

"Um, Prez? If you have the same number of Evil Pieces as a game of chess, then that means you've got another seven Pawns in addition to me, right? So I guess you could have seven more of me on your board..."

There were eight Pawns to a side in chess, so it stood to reason that Rias could have up to eight Pawns in her Familia. *It's probably only a matter of time until she recruits more*, I thought.

However, Rias shook her head. "No. You're my only Pawn, Issei."

—!

Huh? Why do I feel so relieved? Was that a confession? All I need is you, Issei! That kind of thing?

"When a human is reincarnated as a demon, the number of Evil Pieces consumed can vary depending on what special abilities that person has to offer. The more powerful their abilities, the more pieces that are required."

...So it's not a confession... Hold on, consuming pieces?

"In the world of chess, they say Queens are worth nine Pawns, Rooks are worth five, and Knights and Bishops are worth three. These standards are applied to Evil Pieces as well. Moreover, this principle is essential to reincarnation. There are those who would require two Knight pieces to be reincarnated or two Rooks. Moreover, we need to keep in mind an individual's innate affinities. Two different kinds of pieces can't be combined, so a lot of thought has to be put into how they are to be allocated. After all, once used, they can't be taken back."

"What does that have to do with me?"

"Issei, when I reincarnated you, I used all eight of my Pawns. That's what it took to ensure your survival."

All of them? Seriously?! So that means I'm worth eight regular Pawns?

"After I realized how many Pawns you were worth, I simply had to make you my servant. At first, I couldn't quite put my finger on why you cost so much. Now, however, I understand perfectly. You possess the Boosted Gear, one of the sacred, god-destroying Longinuses. It's a Sacred Gear of immense value."

I glanced at my left arm. A red gauntlet, an embodiment of raw power that doubled my strength every ten seconds. If used properly, it could even vanquish God Himself. I couldn't help but think it was too good for me, but given it was already mine, I had no choice but to accept it.

"When I found you, the pieces I had remaining were one Knight, one Rook, one Bishop, and eight Pawns. To reincarnate you as my servant, only all eight Pawns would do the trick. Thankfully, you had a strong affinity with that piece. The others wouldn't have been enough to bring you back. The Promotion ability makes a Pawn's true value a bit of a mystery, so I took a gamble…and won you." Rias broke out into a truly pleased smile. She stroked my cheek with her fingers.

"The Crimson-Haired Princess of Annihilation and the Gauntlet of the Red Dragon Emperor… I don't know if we could be more perfectly matched. Strive to become the mightiest of Pawns. I have complete faith in your abilities, my dear, adorable servant."

The mightiest of Pawns… It had a good ring to it.

Rias brought her face closer to mine. *So close, Prez!* Then she pressed her lips against my brow.

"Just a little spell to strengthen your stamina." She had kissed me on the forehead…

Whoa. I could feel my body growing giddy at this development. Blood rushed to my cheeks. *Whoa. Whoa. Whoooooooaaaaa!* Something snapped inside me. I was so overjoyed, I felt like I could've erupted in celebration!

Seriously! That was my first kiss from a girl! Who cares if it wasn't on my lips or cheek; there was no greater happiness than this! Tears of joy welled up in my eyes! *I-I'll do my best, Prez! I swear it!* I thought.

"But that's enough coddling for now. I wouldn't want our newest member to feel jealous."

Jealous? What's she talking about?

"I-Issei...?" came a familiar voice from behind me.

I turned around only to find a golden-haired beauty—Asia—trying, with limited success, to force a smile.

"A-Asia...?" *Huh? Is she angry with me? Wh-what did I do...?*

"I—I see... I—I understand... P-President Rias is pretty, so it makes sense that you'd like her more... Oh, I shouldn't think things like that! Dear Lord, please forgive my sinful heart—" Asia put her hands together in prayer before suddenly crying out in pain. "I feel like a knife just ran through my head!"

"Of course. God isn't very receptive to the prayers of demons," Rias said matter-of-factly.

"Oh... I see. I'm a demon now. I can't show my face to Him anymore..." Asia's expression clouded slightly.

Come on, there's no need to feel sad! I urged in my mind.

"Do you regret it?" Rias asked her.

Asia shook her head. "Not at all. Thank you. I'm just happy to be with Issei, no matter the circumstances."

I felt my cheeks turning red at that embarrassing response. I mean, I was pleased to hear it, really. It was a huge compliment.

Rias also let out a faint smile. "I see. All is well, then. From now on, you serve me. I have quite a bit of work for you and Issei to do together."

"I'll do my best!" Asia answered enthusiastically.

It would probably just be distributing the leaflets, at least at first. *Will Asia really be okay with that?* Back then, I wasn't so sure. Only then did I realize that Asia looked different. Why had it taken me so long to notice?

"Asia, your clothes..." She was wearing the uniform of Kuou Academy.

"Wh-what do you think...?" she asked nervously.

I could hardly believe it! Another angel had descended from on high to my school! I could already hear all the guys talking about her.

Incredible!

"You look great! Let's take a picture together later!"

"A-ah, okay!"

She really was cute, getting all flustered by my suggestion. It seemed high school life was finally turning my way!

"I have decided that Asia will attend our school from now on," Rias said. "Since she's the same age as you, I've put her in second year—in your class, in fact. Today is her first day, so do make sure to help her out."

Seriously?! My class?! Asia?! I was stunned.

"I'm in your hands, Issei." She bowed her head.

In the back of my mind, I was already imagining how I would introduce her to Matsuda and Motohama. I couldn't stop laughing at the thought of how jealous it would make them.

"Yeah, you can meet my two partners in crime."

"I look forward to it."

Heh-heh. You see that, Matsuda, Motohama? I'm on my way to full adulthood!

Friends, my life as an unpopular high school kid is over! As I lost myself in fantasies, Kiba, Koneko, and Akeno entered the clubroom.

"Good morning, President. Issei. Asia."

"…Good morning… Issei, Asia…"

"How are you this morning, President? And Issei and Asia, too!"

They each greeted us in turn. All three of them had called me by my first name, and they had all acknowledged Asia as a member of our group. It was great! What could've been better?

Rias rose to her feet. "Now that we're all here, let's celebrate!" She snapped her fingers, and with that, a huge cake appeared on the table.

Is this another one of her demonic powers?!

"I—I thought it might be nice to have a little party every now and then, no? W-we have a new member, after all, so I made a cake. Well? Let's eat!" Rias's face had turned red.

A homemade cake! I was overjoyed. *Prez, I swear I'll become the mightiest of all Pawns!*

I'll do my best, together with Asia, Kiba, Koneko, and Akeno! Having made that silent promise, I launched into a Dragon Wave to do my part and hype up the party.

AFTERWORD

The final boss of this book, Dark Satan, the Dragon King of Darkness, bears a deep-rooted enmity against our protagonist. He uses his special move, Dark Breath Type-0, in a ferocious battle against our hero, but our protagonist ultimately wins out thanks to his ultimate move, Chaos Shot. At the end, our hero and heroine elope into the heavens to live happily ever after.

That is how the book finishes.

Ha, I've spoiled it for those of you who skipped to the afterword!

Just kidding. I'm really sorry. Nothing like that happens. I let myself get carried away a little because there are always some people out there who read the afterword before the story itself.

Greetings to my readers old and new. The name is Ichiei Ishibumi. What did you think of *High School DxD*, or *DxD* for short?

It's been two years since I released my last book, so I'm a little nervous. That probably explains why my hand is shaking so terribly and why this afterword got off to such an odd start.

Those of you reading my work for the first time are probably thinking: "What's with this author? All he ever writes about is breasts!" And those of you who have read my works before are no doubt wondering: "Huh? This *is* the horror writer Ishibumi, right? Why the sudden obsession with women's chests?" Well, you know, being an adult is complicated. Think of this as an update to my writing style.

*　　*　　*

Let me lay out my cards up front: I intend for this to be an extremely lively and erotic series. It was actually my editor who first suggested it. "How about we make the main character a lecherous teenager?" Things just kind of snowballed from there, and I'm having so much fun writing it!

Harem series usually revolve around sensitive and insecure young men or a protagonist with a strong sense of justice but who lacks experience with the opposite sex. I thought it would be interesting to see what I could do with a good-for-nothing hero who is absolutely obsessed with picking up girls.

I'm telling the story from Issei's perspective, so the idea is that the readers will want to interrupt and cry out: "No, no, that's wrong! Think about what you're doing for a minute!"

Issei isn't as smart as you all—in fact, he can be a complete and utter fool at times—so please don't be too harsh with him.

Well, it looks like I have a few pages left for this afterword, so how about I touch on my overall vision for the series?

High School DxD is a schoolyard love story, a comedy, a fantasy, and a battle series that follows the escapades and coming-of-age of Issei Hyoudou. That's a bit of a long-winded description, but I'm sure if you know what those genres are all about, you'll get a good idea of what's to come.

The main character, our protagonist, is Issei. The main supporting character and heroine is Rias. Asia is the other heroine. The tale revolves around Issei and these two young women. The three of them will get caught up in the havoc wrecked by the other characters, which include Kiba, Koneko, and Akeno.

The members of the Occult Research Club at Kuou Academy—in other words, the members of Rias Gremory's Familia—go about their demon work while all kinds of crazy antics unfold around them. They'll fight against angels and fallen angels, discover legendary weapons, and encounter fantastical beasts! At least, that's the plan.

The basic concept is that love and dreams and battle are all basic components of youth!

Demons and angels are the main theme, so expect plenty of names from myth and legend to pop up. That said, I'm the one writing this story, so you can look forward to plenty of surprises as well!

Put simply, I might use events and circumstances mentioned in the Bible and other religious sources for reference, but I'm taking liberties to write an original story.

It would be best to enter *High School DxD* knowing that most of the ideas and concepts relating to angels and demons are my own creation. I mean, there's nothing like Evil Pieces in the Bible.

The Great War between the demons, God, and the fallen angels ended several hundred years prior to the beginning of this tale and serves as the backdrop to the current tensions between these three factions. The most famous angels and demons have already passed away by the beginning of the story.

That said, I'm thinking about bringing in plenty of other influences, too. Things from Norse mythology, Japanese mythology, and so forth. In this world that I'm creating, anything is possible!

I'm sure you'll have plenty of questions and expectations regarding Rias's servants.

You might be wondering who her other Bishop is, for example. I've actually already decided with my editor that we'll introduce this character as the series progresses, so I hope you get to meet soon.

So what about the other pieces?

With all her Pawns used up, Rias has one Knight and one Rook left. Just as I plan to introduce the other Bishop in due course, expect these spare pieces to eventually be put to use, too.

Huh? Is that it?

No, not at all. I have it all planned out, so the rest depends on you, my readers.

Whether or not *High School DxD* will continue with a second volume will depend on the sales of this first one. If it does continue, though, expect the erotic tension to build to greater and greater heights! It'll mainly involve Rias and Asia.

I already have a very special something in mind for Volume 2. Let's hope it doesn't go up in smoke. Those of you who want to see more of Rias's breasts, I look forward to your support.

Now then, on to my thanks.

To my former editor, K, who helped develop the scenario for this work, and to H, my current editor, who stood by me from the start as I forged ahead with our plan.

My thanks go out to both of you. We've finally made *High School DxD* a reality. I'm incredibly grateful for everything you've both done.

To Miyama-Zero, my illustrator. Thank you so much for the wonderful pictures. I was incredibly moved the first time I saw your depictions of Rias and Asia—they were just as I had imagined them! Sorry for all the trouble involved perfecting and reworking the characters' appearances and uniforms.

To my fellow authors! Thanks for your encouragement and support each time we went out drinking! Thanks to you all, I managed to get everything back on track! I'm looking forward to the next round!

And lastly, to my friends! Sorry for all the trouble and hardship I caused! I finally managed to release the book! Thanks for looking out for me last year! We'll have to share a meal together again soon!

That's it for now. Once more, to my editors, friends, and fellow authors, thank you.

I'll do my best to see that this series keeps on going!

One other thing—I have a blog I started last year that you can check out. I mostly just write about *Pokémon* and *Gundam*, but I think it would be nice to comment on *DxD* every now and then, too.

*   *   *

It's called Ichibui. You can find it at: http://ishibumi.exblog.jp/

Lastly, I know it's only a few lines, but I have a few words for someone very important to me.

To my father, who passed away while I was writing this first volume:

I finished my book. Sorry for all the stress and worry I caused.

Ichiei Ishibumi

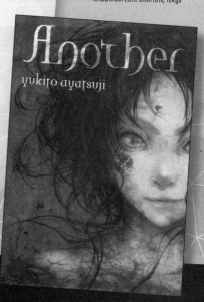

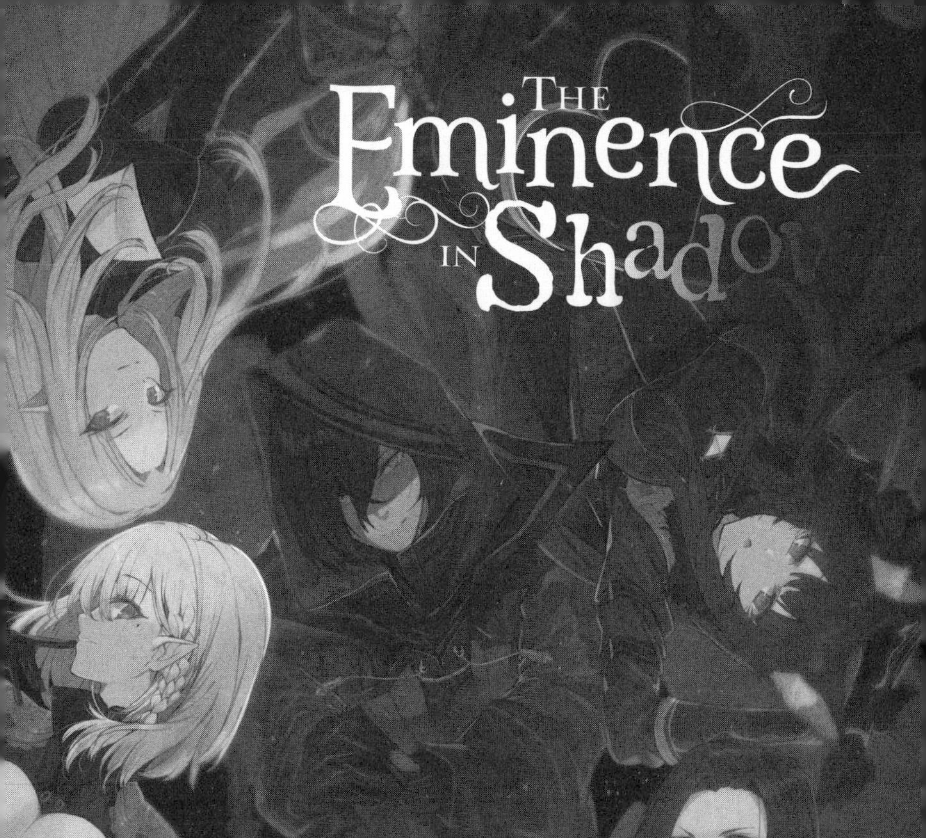
THE
Eminence
IN Shadow

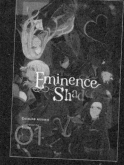